Married Games

By J.F. Lowe

Married Games
J.F. Lowe
Published by Mercurial Publishing
Copyright © 2019 Mercurial Publishing
Edited by Bailey Macks
EBook ISBN: 978-0-6483824-5-4
ISBN: 978-0-6483824-8-5

This is a work of fiction. Names, places, characters and incidents are the product of the author's imagination and are fictitious. Any resemblance to actual persons, living or dead, events or establishments is solely coincidental.

Dedication

To my loving husband, whom none of this would ever be possible without.

Prologue

As the prisms of light filter through our bedroom door, the sound of my husband's light snore beside me bears no comfort. I'm exhausted, but I don't want to close my eyes. It's not that I am afraid. Or maybe I am. But not of my husband, god no. He is the most loving, supportive and caring man I have ever met. I know he loves me, and I am completely and utterly head over heels in love with

Matthew. He is the kind of man that I always wished I could have my happily ever after with.

So what had happened. Why am I laying here wondering what had put me in the hospital? Why had four Victorian Police officers come and searched my house and threatened to take my husband away. Why did I feel like something seriously wrong had occurred. I just don't know. I know that the exhaustion is playing its part.

I watch the rise and fall of my husband's chest; maybe if I concentrate on that, I will fall into a lull and drift off to sleep. But after another hour somehow it's not as comforting as it once was. Instead, my chest feels tight, and my heart continues to race. I force myself to take a deep breath, but the anxiety rises once again. I know something is wrong. Is it me? Did I do something? Did I take something? The emergency doctor had told me my blood alcohol was 0.02 which to me was no that high. With that amount of alcohol in my system, I could still have legally driven a motor vehicle.

We had two bottles of wine between the two of us. A bottle of crisp white Sauvignon Blanc and I had barely finished my first glass of Shiraz. It had been a typical Saturday night. In fact, it was the first Saturday night in months that we had decided to stay in, have a few wines and a nice cheese platter. Cheese and wine had always been our thing. The cheese platter had had all of his favourites, a beautiful Tasmanian blue, a creamy triple Brie and apricot and almond cheese, topped off with my favourite Danish salami and line of plain and peppered crackers on each side of the board. We even had our favourite YouTube playlist running on the television in the lounge room as background noise.

So, why did I end up in hospital? Why did the police come? And why did I feel like our lives have just been turned upside down. I lay watching my husband, no it definitely isn't fear of my husband keeping me awake but maybe more fear of myself. A sinking feeling that I may have just ruined my marriage, my life and hurt the only man I have ever truly loved.

Chapter 1

Sarah

Three Months Earlier…

The keys turn in the front door.
He's home, my love is home. It's only
been eight hours since I last saw him

but each day seems to feel longer. I sit waiting to greet him as he enters our inner city five bedroom penthouse apartment. As the jingle of the keys to play, nothing sounded better than to know he was home. I was not alone anymore. Except for Baxter that is. Baxter our little fur baby, a little seven-month-old Jack Russel that from the moment we went to the breeders home he came right out and licked my foot as if a sign to say, your my human.

I am his human alright, he absolutely ignores all others when it comes to taking orders. He is a people dog but I am the only he will listen to when I tell him to sit or no or basically any other command. Then again, am the only one that he spends all his days with, as he sits by my feet while I either write or read. That where life has come to in my thirty-six year long life. I turned into everything I never thought I would be.

Gone were the days where I was a CEO of a multi-million dollar company living the high life on cruise ships travelling the world and earning a good salary as I went. My life was now isolation, novel characters and wine.

My husband finally enters our apartment,you would never think that he is a construction mogul with the way he places his filthy construction lunch box on the kitchen table. Then again, Matthew is always the hands-on kind of guy. He knows every part of his business inside and out. He still gets on the tools most days, changing out of his suit and into his high vis gear before helping out on site when needed.

Mr reliable is what I called him when we first met. Just like his routine every day when he gets home from work. He kisses me hello before heading to the veranda and disposing of this finished lemonade bottle in the bottle recycling bin. It is the same for his lunch and pretty much everything about my husband. His alarm goes off at five thirty, we both get up. He opens the wardrobe and dresses in his suit for work and I head off to make his lunch. It's the say every week, day. Two ham and cheese wraps with three snack size chocolates and a 1.25 litre bottle of sugar-free lemonade. I use to think that anybody that ate the same thing each day must be a bit strange because have the same monotonous thing would be like eating cardboard.

That was the thing though, ever since meeting my husband two years prior it was always the same. Every day during the week was the same and when he returned home at night it was more of the same. After he returns from the veranda, he kisses me lightly again before retreating to the shower. I had the same routine too. While he showered, I would get up and grab a glass of wine and sit on the couch until he six o'clock when the news starts. I would rise from the couch and begin making dinner.

Day after day during the week, nothing changes and then the weekend is always just as predictable. Saturday morning breakfast out at our local cafe, caramel latte and smashed avocado on toast for me and either pancakes or corn fritters if he was feeling adventurous. After we would go and see an elderly neighbour as she had been placed in a nursing home by her children and then we would either go the local bar or head to a restaurant before heading to the bar later in the evening.

Our lives the same story week after week, like the same song on repeat. The only change we had in our lives was a recent diagnosis of cancer for me. A lump that had appeared in my mouth a month prior to our wedding had grown and now was creating issues with my speech and not to mention ridiculously annoying as it rubs against my teeth. I had thought it was a simple mouth ulcer.

Something that would disappear after the stress of the wedding had

died down. But it hadn't and
eventually it got sick of it and gone to
my local doctor. It took her less than
five minutes before referring me off to
the Ear, Nose and Throat specialist on
a priority list and less than ten days
before I was surgery removing the
cancers.

It was another blow to my health
something that I had to fight with
since the early months of my life.
Another cancer. Another surgery and
another time in my life where the
worry of making it to my next
birthday begins. It was something I
thought about regularly. It feels like
I'm a living and breathing medical
book. I had already learnt how to

cope with the diagnosis after my second cancer diagnosis six years prior, but this time had my husband by my side at every step. That was something I was not use to. I was used to being alone throughout the process.

The doctors, the chemotherapy, radiation and what seemed like never-ending moments of being a pin cushion. Throughout my first two cancers my former husband was never there, no family and no friends. I had been sent to the hospital seven hours away in the capital city and my former sister-in-law sat in the waiting area on the ground floor each and every time I went. But that was always the case.

I became chatty with the medical professions along the way just to keep myself from crying for each procedure. I had developed such a habit that I was on a first name basis with my local phlebotomists at the pathology lab. We made light of the fact that I was there on either a weekly or daily basis depending on the circumstances. I called her my very own vampire. She laughed everything when I said she was more real than Edward from the Twilight Saga. Then again maybe she didn't realise that at the time I just wanted to be immortal or at least be alive long enough to watch my three children grow up, get married and maybe one day make me a grandmother but I never told her that.

This time though I wasn't alone. Matthew sat beside me, holding my hand and gently rubbing my back as we waited in the admission section of the hospital. I'm not sure who was more scared and whether he was holding my hand to console me or if it made him feel better as he didn't speak. I'm not sure quite sure that he could. He had become more animated from the moment I told him that I had cancer. That day played through my head.

I sat patiently in the specialist office and told myself that I might walk away with a few stitches today as surely he would just lance what I thought was a cyst and after the stitches dissolve and I would be back to normal.

That wasn't the case, after a careful examination and nasal camera inserted the specialist who had been all smiles at the beginning of the appointment had become sullen. He was extremely polite but I could tell that he was trying to find the words to tell me it wasn't as simple as I thought. Letting out a deep breath I'm sure he had been holding.

"Sarah, we need to take this out and immediately." He said flipping through his leather bound desk diary.

"I am going to move some things around but I will book the surgery for the morning of the eighteenth. There is no waiting for this and to be honest the severity of it won't be completely clear until I open it up and can do further exploration under general anaesthetic." He finally said as raised his head to finally look at my face.

"Umm, what am I missing here. I thought this was just an ulcer or a cyst that would be over an done with today. "

"Sarah, I believe what you have is a mucoepidermoid carcinoma. Which is a form of cancer that affects the salivary glands. We need to do surgery and straight away."

Bile rose in my throat, cancer. No. Not again. I had already beaten cancer twice first Ewing's sarcoma in my right humerous in 2009 and then medullary carcinoma in my right breast in 2013. It can't be cancer, I can not go through that again. The doctor's voice drowned out by the sound of my heart pounding through my head.

My heart raced and my stomach continued to churn while the rest of my body seemed to be on autopilot. It must have been because I managed to leave the ear, nose and throat specialist and the 35 minutes drive through the city home before the tears finally began to fall.

"Sarah. Sarah." A shaking on my thigh brought me back to the present.

"Sarah, the nurse is here to take you up to pre-op" my husband offered his hand to help me from my seat.

"Oh, I'm sorry." I stood collecting my bag. I turned and gave my husband a kiss before following the nurse through the restricted access area.

Chapter 2

Matthew

I had known that I was all wrong for her, that I never should have touched her, but I'd been so drawn to her sweet innocence, her genuine smiles, her interest in me as a person, that I'd been unable to resist her.

She made me laugh when he'd forgotten how. She made me want to be more when I'd stopped believing in anything good. She'd pulled me out of a grim existence and had given me something to hope for. She'd made me feel when I thought my father's physical and verbal abuse had stripped me of the ability to care for anyone or anything.

She was my salvation, my reason for turning my life around when I had been so close to not giving a shit about anything and probably would have turned out just like my old man if it hadn't been for her giving me something to truly live for.

I had been stuck in a rut of work, sex and booze. My longtime friend Eden had been the only constant in my life but even then our relationship was toxic. We had met at a BDSM club in Melbourne's outer suburbs after I'd received an invitation from a childhood buddy that had gone into the Navy. He and his mates owned the club and offered me a place to relax and learn the lifestyle.

The moment I had met Eden I knew he was trouble, but I couldn't help but look at him with a sense of awe. The way that women seem to flock to him. He was charismatic and

from what I had learnt, a good
dominant. It was only when I walked
past one of the view rooms one
evening that I found out he was a
man that also liked to share women. I
stopped by the window watching him
as he in unison with another man
fucked the woman fifty shades of
Sunday. It was one of the most erotic
things I had ever seen. It was at that
moment Eden's eyes locked with
mine and his silent nod became the
start of a long friendship.

We shared many women of
the next five years, some as one-night
stands and others became more long
term. None of them stayed though.
They always ended up telling me that

they only really wanted Eden. So, I was back to being alone. That was until the day I met Sarah.

She had sent through a request to the construction company I worked for at the time for a quote on bathroom renovations on her inner-city apartment. I had turned up early as usual and grabbed a coffee before heading up to her apartment. When I arrived, the door had been slightly ajar. I knocked but no answer. I called out but no response. I stepped into the apartment and that's when I saw her. Headphones on in front of her laptop, in an oversized shirt white shirt, what appeared to be braless and the most granny like underwear I think I had ever seen. She was the most gorgeous woman I had ever seen.

Her foot tapping a way to whatever she was listening to which made her breast bounce. I couldn't help but stare. I watched as she picked up her glass of water absentmindedly before missing mouth completely and spilling it down her front.

She jumped from her chair. I couldn't help myself I had to laugh. She was the sexiest and clumsiest person I'd ever seen. It must be my laugh that alerted her to the fact she wasn't alone. When she turned she shrieked. My mouth went dry and I was instantly hard. It was like the wet T-shirt competition of my dreams. The beautiful full globes on full display through the wet shirt. I stepped back with my hands up to show I wasn't going to hurt her or some creepy stalker.

"I'm sorry the door was open. I'm Matthew Davidson, I have an appointment to quote on the bathroom" I stammered.

It was then she seemed to remember that she was half naked trying to cover herself with her hands. No matter how much she tried to cover the wet shirt showed everything, but I wasn't exactly going to point that out because I'm sure if

she looked at me properly, she would
have noticed the tent in my pants.

"Oh, shit. That's today," she
finally said.

"Yes, eleven o'clock." I
replied trying to hide my amusement
at the scene in front of me.

"Umm, can you give me a
minute. I'll be right back" she turned
and disappeared.

That was the day I knew
Sarah would one day become my
wife. Two years later she did.

Now we were both
successful in our own right, Sarah
with her training company and then
becoming a Best Seller novelist. I had
landed on my feet after meeting her

and seeing that anything is possible
no matter what crap cards life had
given you as a child. A shiver of
horror ran through me at the thought
of my childhood. My father had
abused my mother and by the time I
was eight he had decided that I was
fair game too. That was until the day
he finally went too far and killed my
mother by throwing her into a wall
one too many times and gotten a life
sentence for murder.

God, I wish my mother had
the strength that my wife did. My
wife never gave up, she just grinned
and said that only the good die young
and there was no way cancer would
stop her. Matthew sighed, it may not

stop her but this being her third cancer certainly is taking its toll.

Initially we thought nothing of it. It was just a small lump that we thought was an ulcer that showed up about the same time as her mother did for our wedding. She laughed it off saying, "I'm glad it's only a mouth ulcer and not a stomach ulcer because spending a week with my mother is bound to give anyone an ulcer."

After that we thought nothing of it. It was only when her speech slowly started to change that she finally went to the doctors. Now I'm sitting in the family waiting room until she finishes surgery.

I got up from my seat again

and started pacing. Why is this taking
so long? It's been two hours already
and they said she would be out by
now. I check my phone. Nope
nothing. No calls from recovery and
no one had come out to get me yet. As
I stride up to the nurse's desk the
nurse holds her hand up me.

"Mr Davidson, it has only
been a few minutes since you last
asked, I don't have any news yet. I
will let you know when I have
information. Please take a seat. Or
better yet the hospital cafe is just
down the hall if you would like
something. I will come and get you if
something changes."

"Fine" I grunt before

turning towards the hall.

Eden, how are you? I was wondering if you could do me a favour. I'm looking for a new car for my wife."

"Ah the illustrious Sarah, I am yet to meet. I would have meet her at your wedding if you hadn't eloped"

"Yeah, yeah you knew why, she said she would do anything to keep things from the press and her mother." I said in jest, but it was partly true the press had been following them since they had been listed as Melbourne's new power couple. Her mother was a handful but nothing compared to his family.

"So, what's on the cards my friend, something sporty fun to ride like the old days? Or are you a kept man these days and need practical?"

"Actually, I'm thinking the latest Mazda CX-8, if you have any on hand. I'd like to have it in the next week or two." Not that I was telling him, but I was hoping it would become a family car for us as my work dual cab ute wasn't exactly suitable for a baby seat. I never thought I would be thinking about having a child of my own but that was Sarah. She gave me hope of having a family that I never had. I looked at my watch again and another fifteen minutes had passed. I need to find out what the hell was taking so long with Sarah's operation.

"Look mate I have to get going, flick me through an email with model details and colour." I wasn't sharing with Eden what was happening. Him further involved in our lives could only end one way. I brushed the errant thoughts of Eden aside as I stalked back to the nurse's desk.

Chapter 3

Sarah

Bloody hell that sound is annoying. I wish someone would turn off that beeping. The sound drowns out again.

BEEP... BEEP ...BEEP.

I reach my hand out to swat the alarm.

"Ahh, your awake" my eyes adjust the bright lights overhead to make out the nurse beside the hospital bed.

"You're in post-op, love, the surgeon will be by shortly to tell you how it went" she said leaning over and pressing a button that finally put an end to the god-awful beeping. I try to reply but my mouth doesn't seem to want to work. Noise came out but sounded nothing like words.

"Don't speak, love. Your lips and mouth are swollen. I will grab a face pack and see if we can get that inflammation down." The nurse jotted some notes in what appeared to be my chart before walking off. Bringing my hand up to my lips, I could feel what she could obviously see. Shit. I must look like a cross between Bubba from Forest Gump and a chipmunk because it all felt swollen.

"We have called your husband to let him know you are in post-op, he should be here any minute now." While she spoke, the nurse attaches a jock strap device filled with ice. "Now you be sure to let me know if you're in any pain as we want to nip that in the bud straight away."

I try to speak again, this time concentrating on the movement of my mouth.

"Water" barely a whisper from my lips but yet the smile from the nurse told me that she knew exactly what I wanted, and she left once again returning almost immediately with a white plastic cup. As she lifted the cup to my mouth, "Sip it, slowly" the coolness of the water tingled across my lips. Just the smallest of sips was thirst quenching.

I hear him before I see him. The shuffle of feet and the "where is she." He's angry. What happened to make him angry. I can hear it in his voice. Oh god, how long was I in surgery for? Maybe he's been in the waiting room all this time. The curtain pushes back and my specialist motions for my husband to walk past him and into the cubicle.

"Finally, anyone would think you people are trying to keep me from my wife," he huffed walk to the side of the bed and placing his hand on my shoulder.

"Mr Davidson, we are merely following hospital protocol and only allowing loved ones in once the patient is awake and stable" the doctor shook his head before lifting up the chart from the hospital bedpost.

Chapter 4

Matthew

Thankfully Sarah's surgery had gone well and I was able to take her home the next morning. The next few days I spent working from home so that I could be there for Sarah. It felt strange, I had never had to care for anyone other myself full time my entire life. But it was all worth it. Sarah is and always will be the love of my life. She may not be the first woman I ever had but she will certainly be the last.

I made soup and anything I could make that she could drink through a straw thanks to her swollen lip and made midnight trips to the twenty-four-hour takeaway store for ice cream to help reduce the swelling. Thankfully after a few days the swell had reduced, and Sarah was feeling much better.

What was the best news though

was the call we had been waiting for
from the Ear, Nose and Throat
surgeon that they had a clear margin
on all fifteen tumours they removed.
Also, that no positive nodes were
present. All which Sarah explained to
me as being a fantastic result and that
chemotherapy and radiation therapy
would not be required.

I breathed a sigh of relief. The
tension that had me wound up like a
coil had finally lifted. There of course
is always a chance that the cancer
might return but I couldn't think of
that. I had to stay positive. I had to be
positive for Sarah even if the thought
of it all scared the living daylights out
of me.

Sarah seemed to just smile and take it in her stride but as always that was my wife. Strong.

I wanted to celebrate. Sarah just acted as if it was another day but what she hadn't known is that I had a surprise waiting for her. I'd organised it while she was in hospital and only hoped she loved the new car. Now I had to find a way to her. I wasn't the biggest romantic but for Sarah I would try anything to show her how much I love her.

"What's the plan?" She asked stepping out into the hallway.

"First, a picnic lunch." I held up a basket. She gave him a dubious look and she laughed, her eyes sparkling.

"Don't worry, I figured you might need something gentle relaxing after the past few weeks."

A grin broke across her face and I could see a bit of relief in her smile. I wondered if she thought I was going to make things out to be more than they were. The cancer scare was over and she didn't need to worry about that.

"Where are we going for our picnic?" She asked.

"To one of your favourite places," I said with a grin. I knew how much she owed this place but she a look he gave me was almost shy. We walked without talking, letting the sounds of the city be the only noise between us.

I'd always considered myself a city guy, but there were cities and then there were cities; I hadn't realised how different Melbourne was than other places until I saw it from Sarah's perspective.

When I turned, Sarah realised where we were going and smiled. Aside from the library, one of her favourite places to go was Carlton Gardens. With all of its historical buildings, sculptures and fountain made it one of the city's favourite romantic spots. Not that I'd come here much.

Sarah turned my attention back to me.

"On the really hot days, I used to

take my shoes off and go wading in the water to cool off." She laughed.

I couldn't help but laugh too, as I could imagine her sitting on the edge of the fountain, book in hand and enjoying the sunshine.

I reached over and threaded my fingers through hers and we picked a spot under a couple trees and I spread a tablecloth on the grass. Sarah sat down and watched as I opened the basket.

"You know I'm not great at the romantic thing, so you can't laugh at anything I brought."

She agreed, amused, but not for the reason she probably would've thought. I'd never considered how some things I took for granted, Sarah did everything when it came to meals. Sarah could see I actually managed a decent selection, including some mild cheese, crackers and fruit. I'd also brought nice bottle of red hoping that it would help with my other surprise the car.

"When I told you this morning that I wanted to take you out, this probably wasn't what you'd had in mind, was it?" I asked as I began to pack up the leftovers.

"No, it wasn't," she answered honestly. Sarah frowned and she looked down. She put her hand on my wrist, immediately understanding how I'd taken my statement.

"It was better."

"You're really saying you aren't disappointed that I took you here with a picnic lunch instead of to some fancy restaurant?"

"Are you kidding?" She leaned closer to me, enjoying the smell of her floral perfume. "That's the sweetest thing anyone's ever done for me."

"Well then I hope that this is even better." Sheepishly I pulled the Mazda brochure from the bottom of the basket and hand it to Sarah. "You have to go and pick up the new car from the Mazda dealer, the salesman will be ready for you at any time after Tuesday."

Sarah squealed and lunched

herself towards me landing kisses all over my face. I couldn't help but laugh before rolling her underneath me and taking the kiss I really wanted.

Chapter 5

Sarah

I sat at the car dealership waiting for the salesman to finish with his current customer. Eden, he seemed like a nice enough guy but he seemed to work at a snail's pace all the time.

Matthew had said that all she had to do was go in and sign the papers. It was supposed to be her new car, but there was nothing about the car that I had picked. I had wanted something small and zippy and Matthew wanted practical with all the bells and whistles. So really it was a car for him. A new Mazda CX-8, with a new skyactiv-d 2.2L Diesel engine, smart city brake support and 19-inch alloy wheels. Everything he wanted, right down to the black metallic paint colour and the dark russet Napa leather seats.

The salesman made his way towards me, his small stature giving no hint the sarcastic wit that came out of the man's mouth.

"Well hello, Sarah. A pleasure to meet you finally." I had started to wonder if his greetings had a double meaning as he had always tending to linger on the phone when he had called to set up the details about the car and the car delivery pickup at the dealership. This time he lingered when shaking my hand. It's not that he was being inappropriate but he seemed to check her out and get an all too knowing smile as he greeted me. It was like he knew me without meeting me in person ever.

"Matthew tells me you will be taking delivery of the car this morning."

"Ah yes, he said you have some paperwork for me?"

"Absolutely, come this way." The salesman motioned towards the far office which I assumed is his. As we go through the forms, the vehicle registration, insurance and sales sheet the salesman points out the various details and required signatures. Nothing that I hadn't expected except for the little touches each time that he handed his pen to sign. Feeling like touches becoming more deliberate. Just when I begin to question how much more paperwork is required Eden suddenly stands.

"Shall I take you through the features of the and a quick drive so you feel comfortable with the car before heading home?"

"Sure"

The salesman leads me towards the sign new black metallic Mazda CX-8 and opens the drivers side door before motioning me to take a seat. Leaning into the vehicle and begins to point out the various features on the steering wheel. The cruise control, Blue-tooth control functions and music settings. He stretches across in front of me brushing my breast with his arm in to point out the centre console features and then brushes past them again Retreating to stand back straight beside the open driver's door. His pants now tented with his erection and he makes no attempt to hide it. What was with this guy. Is this what he does to all women car buyers?

"You know Sarah, I have known Matthew many years now and never said anything about how beautiful you are. You really are lovely."

He knows Matthew? Since when? Why had Matthew had never mentioned him before.

"Oh, I didn't realise you knew Matthew prior to now"

"At least twenty years now. Stay where you are, I will pop in the other side and take you through the sat navigation system."

The salesman Eden rounded the

car and sat in the passenger seat beside me. There is something off with this guy. I'm missing something. He gives me a feeling that I'm not sure I like. It's as if he knows something more about me then a car salesman should. As my brain trays to mull over the new information about Matthew the salesman shows me through the navigation system.

"Shall we take you for a spin before I let you go off on your own?" he says leaning over once again pressing a button place at my knee height. His hand lingers for a moment as I sit startled and wishing I hadn't worn such a short skirt. His eyes never leave me, it is as if watching to see my reactions. I place my foot on the brake and place the car into drive before easing out of the car lot.

"Where do you want me to take it?" I asked hoping that he would opt for just a quick drive around the block to prove that I could hand the car before leaving.

"Mm, there are so many places" he grinned again.

"Are you always such a cocky prick?"

His deep laugh fills the car and flush of embarrassment reddens my cheeks. "I can see why Matthew married you now. Smart, sexy and a complete brat. And as for cocky Sarah you have no idea."

I dive the car around the block and quickly returned the car lot.

"Your all good to go Sarah. Enjoy the new car. Oh, and Sarah do behave now. You wouldn't want to get in trouble with Matthew."

I turn to tell him off, but he is already exiting the car. I shake my head, thank goodness that was over. It was all a bit weird, let alone creepy. His words run through my head again. Shit would I get in trouble from Matthew ? Shit, was I rude?

Chapter 6

Matthew

My phone dinged and I swiped the message open. Eden.

You have a lovely sub - E

You' re talking about my wife - M

**Why haven't you brought her to
the club so we could share? - E**

**You know why, she's innocent
and I'd like to keep it that way - M**

The rest of the day I was restless.
I'd knew I had been an idiot to let
Sarah go and collect the car but the
car was hers, so I thought it was the
right thing to do at the time. Eden.
Fucking prick. He knew I would react
like this. I tried to suppress the growl
in my throat.

Sarah is mine. My wife. Mine.

It was as if I was trying to

convince myself of things I already knew. I couldn't help it. When it came to Eden being near my wife, I felt like a child that a bully is trying to steal their toy.

"Mine" I growled.

"Sorry Sir, can I help you with something." Jeanette's voice pulling me from my jealousy.

"Shit, sorry Jeanette, I hadn't seen you standing there." God how much had she hear. Did I say it all out loud or just the last part? Fuck. I didn't want to scare her off. She had only worked for me for the past six months and actually seemed to have a brain in her head not like the one they'd sent over from the temp agency.

"It's, okay, Sir. I get possessive about things I belong to me too." Her voice reassuring that I hadn't gone too far. anything you need Sir, I'm always here for you" her heels clicking along the floor as she exited my office.

I shook my head in disgust at myself. I really need to get control of my emotions. No better yet control when it comes to Sarah. I need her to know she's mine. I will not share her.

I closed down my computer and headed home. There was only one way this was going to work, and it had to start today.

*****

I watched as Sarah came through the garage door, the sway of her hips, her beautiful lush arse. The things I would love to do that arse. After the massages from my old friend I couldn't help myself. Mine.

My kiss was unapologetically rough, brutal possessive, but that was the side of me, my wife had never seen. I could see that it rocked her to the core and set her on fire. My firm lips pushed hers apart and my tongue thrust inside, delving deep and claiming her mouth in a way that declared, you are mine. She could taste his hunger, could feel his rising need, even as I maintained complete control of her like always. Cool, calm and controlled. I needed to be if I planned on keeping her from Eden.

I pressed the button for the garage door to close, and begin kissing my way down my wife's neck, I love the way she shivers under my hot breath. Her nipples visible through the thin film of her white blouse. Time to see if she how Sarah responds to the real me.

Chapter 7

Sarah

I arrived home to find Matthew already in the garage leaning against his tool bench. Had Eden already called him? And what is going on with my husband, I had never seen him so possessive. The way that he kissed me and the way we made love right there on his tool bench in the garage. It was hot. I definitely want more of where that came from. Sex with my husband was usually great and by god he has a fantastic cock. Long and thick veined shaft and bulbous head that I love to get my mouth on but there was something different about it. It was like he was trying to mark me as his.

He unzipped my skirt at the side and taking my underwear with one tug he let them float to the floor.

"Your fuck gorgeous" his words sent a rush of desire through me

unlike anything I've ever felt before —
until his palm slides between my legs
and cups me before dragging a single
thick finger through my wetness.
Matthew groaned. Pure male, husky.

"You're fucking drenched for me.
Jesus."

His fingertip swirls my opening,
teasing me. My thighs flex, and when
he dips just barely inside, my inner
walls clench, greedy and wanting to
be filled. What is happening to me? I
push myself against his hand, and for
a moment, he fills me. His hand drops
away, and a cool rush of air precedes
a light slap to my pussy.

"Wha—"

"My greedy wife is getting ahead

of herself. I'll give you what you need, but you'll take it my way."

When I exhale sharply, another firmer smack lands in the same spot. And then he grips my hips and flips me onto my back in a single movement. My head is still spinning from the abrupt change in position, but my eyes track him as he leaves the edge of the tool bench, moves toward the tool stand box, crouches low, and then returns. He kneels at the base of the metal bench, grips my knees, and pulls me so my ass is almost hanging off the edge and my stilettos are resting on his shoulders. I'm completely and utterly exposed to him, and uncertainty fills me for a breath. He lifts something, and in the dim light of the garage, zippy ties.

I don't have time to question, because within moments he ties my ankles to the legs of the bench.

"I thought we might celebrate our new car with a bottle of wine" he says picking up a glass I hadn't noticed. It can't of been there long as glass was still frosted. Matthew lifted the glass to my lips. Mmm crisp white Sauvignon Blanc. Matthew took a sip for himself kissed me again. The mix of cool wine and his hot mouth, furthering my need.

With a grin Matthew leant back, "would you like more wine Sarah?"

"Please" not quite a beg but a plea

for more. I watched Matthew take the bottle expecting him to refill the empty wine glass instead crouches down his mouth inches from my sex. His breath hot against my skin.

Suddenly, chilly liquid hits me and trickles down . . . into his mouth. He catches the wine on his tongue, lapping up my wetness at the same time. Oh my God. Oh my God. Pleasure spikes through me as he sucks and nips and licks until I can't help but lift my hips and buck against his mouth, wanting more and more of this sensation. He stills, the pulsing in my pussy stops, and he lifts his mouth away.

"Wh—"

"You're not going to come until I give you permission. I'm going to enjoy my appetiser first."

My nipples pucker, and arousal raises goosebumps along every inch of my skin.

"Okay," I whisper.

"Please don't stop. Please." I don't know who this senseless creature is who's begging her husband to keep lavishing on her lady bits, but I honestly don't care. I expect him to resume his actions, but he does something else, something completely unexpected.

His dark eyes are locked on mine as he continues to thrust in and out with his finger and lowers his mouth to my clit. And he feasts. I'm riding high on the wave toward orgasm when a second finger pushes inside me for a moment before sliding lower. I flinch against the foreign feeling as his fingertip circles the pucker of my ass. I open my mouth to protest, but the sensation falls away and is replaced by his teeth nipping at my clit.

A moan rips from my throat as an orgasm rips through my body.

When I blink my eyes open, he's standing over me. He must have cut the ties on my legs from bench, even though I didn't realise it. His belt is undone, his pants are unzipped, and his hand is wrapped around a giant cock.

In a swift move I was impaled on his cock. A low groan came from Matthew's throat.

"Your, fucking mine," he repeated over and over again as ploughed into me. My head was spinning at the side to Matthew I had never seen before until he places his thumb between us pressing on my clit sending me over the edge once more.

Chapter 8

Matthew

As I climbed in bed that night next to Sarah, I knew she had been suspicious about the way that I had acted in the garage but I needed her. The way I needed to mark her as mine. I couldn't help myself, the thought of her near Eden had eaten at me all day. I had lost every woman I ever had feelings for to him and to have Sarah in the same proximity as him made my dominant side come out its three-year hiatus. The luckily though my actions hadn't seemed to frighten Sarah off, like I had thought it once would. Maybe the past two years together had changed things, I know it had changed me. I could no longer hold back who I really am.

It not that I wanted to dominate every aspect of her life, not that Sarah would allow that anyway but when it came to what we did in the bedroom. I needed to be in control especially when it comes to dealing with Eden.

Tomorrow Sarah would start seeing the real me.

Chapter 9

Sarah

I woke to my husband's hand draped across my body and his rigid cock against my rear. His fingers slowly making circles around my now peaked nipples through my singlet top. There was no doubt in what my husband wanted.

"Good you're awake"

"Good morning to you too," I said wriggling my arse against him.

"Get on all fours" his instructors clear that he wanted me right then and there. So much for foreplay. Then again how long had he been playing with my nipples. Before I could manage to sit up he spoke again.

"I'm not going to ask again, Sarah."

God what's was eating him today. Surely morning sex would make a man happy. I scrambled to the side of the bed and removed my pathetic excuse for underwear. They were always the type of underwear that would put Bridget Jones to shame with. Practical that was always me. I placed my hands and knees on the bed waiting to feel my husband's fantastic cock.

He ran his hand gently over the curve of arse before skimming over my dampening pussy. "Today your going be good today, aren't you Sarah?"

Smack.Smack. Smack.

His hand came down like rapid fire over my bare arse cheeks. Never once hitting the same place.

"Answer me Sarah"

Smack. Smack. Smack again. Fuck what the hell was happening. What had he said? My arse was stingy, but the heat seemed to seep into my bones and dampen my pussy further.

"Sarah, I won't ask again" his voice harsher and deeper than I had ever heard in the two years we had lived together.

I struggled to get my brain to function, it felt so good but so wrong and what had he asked. Oh.

"Um, yes. I will be good" I finally mumbled trying to work out what was going on.

His fingers slid between my legs, with two fingers thrust into my saturated pussy.

"That's good Sarah, I like it when you do as your told. Now tell me, do like my fingers inside you. Did you like the spanking?"

It was hard to concentrate. His fingers filling me. It felt so good. I'm so close. Oh, please just a little more. Suddenly, I felt empty and the rapid-fire returned. Another five swats.

"Seems like you only respond to me when I spank you, Sarah."

Fuck.

"Yes, yes I like it."

"Good, now I want you to ask for another spanking and put Sir on the end." I was aching, aching for his finger in my pussy again or better yet his cock. God I loved his cock. Thick, long and straining towards his stomach. Just looking at it made me want to take in my mouth, licking and sucking it.

"Please can you spank me again, Sir."

I felt the smooth head of his cock run down the crease of my arse, stopping momentarily at the place where he'd been touching just moments ago before sliding lower, where she was wet, swollen, and incredibly sensitive from my orgasm. He slid slowly inside me, but once he was buried to the hilt, he exhaled a raw groan, grabbed my waist, and began thrusting in earnest.

For long moments, I twisted in his grip, like a marionette dancing for a puppet master as he prolonged the ecstasy.

Chapter 10

Matthew

My discipline finally snapped as she wriggled her arse against my ridgid cock in bed this morning. With an unrefined curse I'd moved over her completely, pressing my chest against her back and burying my face against her neck, claiming her in a wholly primitive, ruthless way.

By god, did I love the way Sarah had responded. I felt like the supreme puppet master with the way she moved and beg to come. Her body mine.

I'd left her sleeping as I got up and showered. I had meeting in the city at ten and needed to slip by the office for the plans before making my way over to the meeting.

I leant over and kissed her head as I left and could only hope that Sarah lost interested in my past in Eden.

Chapter 11

Sarah

I woke to find that Matthew left for work already. I knew he'd been busy on the proposal for the new high rise so I wasn't surprised to find him gone. I went about my usual morning

routine. A fresh banana and coffee.
The life of an author I laughed to
myself as sat down at my office desk.

I was still curious to know why
Eden had said he had known
Matthew for almost twenty years and
yet until buying this new car I had
never heard of him before. I brought
up safari on my MacBook. Time find
out who this Eden is. As she typed in
his name into the search engine an
array of photos popped up.

I scrolled through the photos,
jackpot. Eden Cambridge. I clicked on
the photo and a news article opened.

Millionaire Car Salesman
Playboy Antics

Eden Cambridge a car
salesman from Melbourne 's
elite car yard has turn
selling cars into
sexcapades . With the well -
known playboy caught on
camera having what only
could be described as kink
sex in front of customers
during the delivery of a
car.

Onlookers were caught off
guard by the midday romp as
others cheered when the
woman customer clearly the
full service of her

delivery. Eden Cambridge or as known in some circles as Master E, declined to comment on his actions. The customer who wishes not t   o be named stated that "the best customer service she had ever received."

Well that explains the car salesman's cock attitude towards me. I exited the article and continued to scroll through the photos until my breath caught. Matthew. The picture showed a woman a provocative pose between Matthew and Eden. I clicked on the picture to open it but it wouldn't expand. Please enter your login. Login for what? I exited the photo and clicked it again. To reset password please contact Highclere administrators.

After a few more clicks and multiple tabs open on safari, I finally a page about Highclere. I sat and stared at my screen. Highclere is a BDSM club right here in Melbourne. How did I not know this place existed?

If Matthew was photographed there does that mean? Oh my god is Matthew?

No, there was no way Matthew could have been a submissive for someone like Eden. Maybe Eden was? No, that can't be right either there was a woman in the picture, did they share?

My heart raced. Was Matthew the same man I married? Did he have a need to control, to dominate, to make me submit. Is that why he had been acting so strange the last couple of weeks?

I continued to stare at the picture of Matthew and Eden. Who is this woman? Does he still want her?

Whoever this woman was, she was the opposite of me. Her black dress clung to her slim body and her auburn hair was swept up into an elegant bun. Her makeup was smoky that made her look like a Hollywood starlet. I was nothing compared to this woman. God, look at me I thought. I could certainly use to lose a few kilos and I had Blondie hair and glasses in a really book nerd kind of way.

As I continued to stare at the photo, is that what Matthew really wanted in a wife? I had to admit, though, as my heart slowly climbed back into my chest, she was hot. Sophistication on a stick.

"It's was a long time ago" Matthew's voice came from behind me.

Shit. How much did he see? Did he hear me talking to myself too? I slapped closed my MacBook screen.

"Oh, I…" I didn't have an excuse.

He saw what I was looking at. What could I say, hey my husband of the past few years I was just checking on your old hook-ups. Even to me I sounded crazy and jealous. But I hadn't known that I was going to find that picture. It was just there. What I really wanted to know is why Matthew never mentioned any of it before.

"Sarah, you should really leave the past in the past. It only causes trouble by reliving old memories." He leant over and kissed me on the top of my hair.

"You were a dom?" the question popped out before I could filter.

Matthew you stepped back and

lent against the door frame of my office. As he seemed to mull over his answer a slight smirk crossed lips.

"Let's just say in a former life I was," Matthew's voice seemed to deepen to a level I had never hear before.

There was so much I didn't know about him, this man who I had promised to spend the rest of my life with, to bond myself to him in a way that was irreversible.

"Why didn't you tell me before?"

"Enough Sarah, I don't want to talk about it" he didn't yell but his voice made me feel like I was a child again. I stood and lent against my desk not sure I liked feeling so small.

"Fine, I will look it up. You know I'm good with research." I smiled to myself as I knew I would find out one way or another but I would have preferred to hear it from him. How could our marriage work if he wouldn't let me in? Be patient, I told myself.

"No, you won't" he said stepping forward lifting me to sit on the edge of the desk.

"And what's the big bad dom going to do about it?" I teased.

"Well," he said.

He moved closer to me, his hands wrapping around my waist, pushing his body into mine. "It means there will be consequences."

"Consequences to what, Matthew?"

I could feel my pussy getting wet just from the words he was saying, just from the mere suggestion that he would punish me at work.

"To disobeying me." His lips touched my skin, sliding over the hollow of my throat.

"What kind of consequences?" I moaned.

"Spankings." His hands reached down and unbuttoned my jeans, his fingers sliding against my belly. "This morning's was for pleasure, not discipline"

"Whippings." He tugged them down in the back so that my arse was exposed.

"Floggings." I moaned again as he grabbed my hips.

"Turn around, Sarah," he barked. "And bend over."

I did it immediately, bracing myself on my solid mahogany desk that was sitting on the only seconds before. He slapped me on the backside with his hand, hard and I cried out.

"You've disobeyed me," he said, and I knew he was talking about. I had googled Eden.

"And now there will be consequences."

"Yes, Matthew," I cried as another stinging slap hit my arse. He continued to spank me, harder and harder, his hand moving between my cheeks until they were red and sore, and my pussy was vibrating with need.

"Stand up and turn around," he growled, and I did as I was told. He stared at me, his chest heaving. His hair was damp from the rain that had been coming down in buckets all day throughout Melbourne. Matthew grinned at me devilishly, like he was deciding just what kind of exquisite torture he was about to inflict.

"Take down your pants." I slid my jeans down to my ankles, then paused, awaiting further instructions.

"All the way." I stepped out of

them.

"Now your shirt." I reached down and grabbed the bottom of my shirt and began pulling it up, the cool air conditioning hitting my torso and causing me to shiver.

Chapter 12

Matthew

I felt like a bastard. I was using sex to control my wife. Had promised my self that I wouldn't do it but when I found that she had disobey my implicit instructions about Eden. Why couldn't she leave it alone. I didn't want her looking up Eden, let alone my past.

Maybe I need to show her more of who I use to be. Made Sarah needed it.

My internal battle continue throughout dinner. I helped clean up and went and showered before settling on the couch beside her.

Turning to her I arched my eyebrow.

"Another finding love reality show, really." I honestly didn't care but it was always fun to watch her squirm when I made fun of romance shows.

"Think of it as research for me,

how not to write a romance story" she laughed before leaning in.

She slid her tongue across my lower lip, one hand resting on my knee as my mouth opened. The kiss deepened for several wonderful seconds before she drew back. Her mouth was pure sin, her skin rich silk. And when I pulled her onto my lap, she curled her body around mine like we'd been made for each other.

Gripping her lush ass in my hands, I pulled her closer, felt her breasts press against my chest.

This was crazy.

Insane. I fisted my hand in her hair and tugged, drawing her back away from me. Her breath hitched. The innocence in her reaction had me hard instantly.

Fuck, I needed her.

Chapter 13

Sarah

I was tired of feeling like shit. I was tired of feeling all the bad things, honestly. The ups and downs of the past few months were taking a toll and right now, in Mathew's arms, I wanted to forget about everything except him. He made me feel wanted.

Special.

I shifted on his lap. Between my legs I could feel him grow harder and heat spread through my body, as my pussy pulsed with need. My nipples tightened when I rocked my hips and he sucked in a harsh breath.

He trailed his lips up my neck, took my diamond stud in his mouth, and bit my earlobe gently. I let a moan escape my lips and my body tensed in anticipation.

"You like this" not really a question but a statement as I shivered with delight.

His mouth claimed mine, firm and

insistent, his tongue hot and demanding as he deepened the kiss. I moaned softly.

His fingers tightened at my waist and the other hand slid around to my chest. Tonight, I just wanted. When he brushed over the rigid peak through of my thin cotton shirt, making me arch and moan. There was so much we had been through already, but this, the way he made me feel, was like he is I all that I need. And all that I wanted. I wanted Matthew.

"Matthew," I said on a soft groan.

"That sexy little moan you make drives me fucking crazy," he growled in my ear. Then his hands dug into

my hips and holding me in place
while he grinds against me.

"Are you going to tell me yet how
you know Eden?'

"No" was his only reply.

"You feel so good," I murmured,
resting her hands on his shoulders to
brace herself over him. In this
position, I was a little higher than
Matthew so I could lean down and
pressed her lips to his. His tongue
swept into my mouth and he
wrapped his arms around me back,
pulling me tight against his chest.
Locked into place I couldn't move,
and a frustrated whimper bubbled
from my throat. He swallowed it with
a groan.

He devoured my mouth, sweeping his tongue inside with broad hard strokes. I tried to move my hips, to ease the ache that was pulsing between my legs but he held me firm. I growled and the damn man chuckled before pulling his head back and burying his mouth in my neck. His teeth nipped along the sensitive column, making my entire body break out in goose bumps. When I tried to move my legs, his arms locked I tighter against his body. He held my immobile, running his teeth than his tongue over my neck, up under my ear.

"Damn you," I panted. No matter how hard I tried I couldn't get any friction where I needed it. I was hot and wet and so ready for him.

"Matthew, please."

"Fuck," he growled. He dragged his lips back to my mouth and took mine in a hungry, toe curling kiss.

"Maybe we should go to our bedroom?" he managed to get out.

"Or maybe we can both stop playing games and see what happens," I told him.

His dark chuckle only fuelled the fire burning in my gut. Fine, he wanted to play dirty, I would play dirty. I leaned away from him just enough to reach the hem of my shirt and before he knew what I was doing, pulled it over my head. I hadn't put on a bra earlier.

My nipples tightened as they brushed over his shirt covered chest and I arched back, dragging them back and forth slowly.

"Fuck," he muttered, his dark gaze lowering.

His tongue came out and he ran it over his bottom lip. Liquid heat pooled between my legs and my nipples got even harder. Every harsh breath out of his mouth made his chest rise and I moved back and forth against him. He either had to let my hips go so he could touch me or I would keep rubbing against him and drive him crazier.

A low groan ripped from my

throat when I moved the hard tips over him. Maybe my plan had a flaw or two. Thankfully, Matthew loosened one arm and slid it up my side, around the front to cup my breast. When he rolled my nipple between his thumb and finger, my head fell back and I dug my nails into his shoulders. Sparks ignited and grew hotter, making a fiery trail through my veins. I had enough room to rock enough to feel him and I could feel my stomach muscles tighten.

God, I was going to get off riding him fully clothed.

"Matthew" my strangled plea fell from my lips and his jaw grew hard, but his body went harder. He loosened his other arm and slid his free hand down the front of my pants, not hesitating before he sank two fingers inside my wet core. I pushed myself up and down onto his fingers and when he crooked them just enough and pressed his thumb against my clit, raw blinding pleasure burst apart inside me so fast that I forgot how to breathe. A long low moan ripped from my throat as I clenched around his hand, my hips still rocking back and forth.

"Fucking hell, Sarah," he growled. His chest rose and fell rapidly and his fingers still moved inside me. The edge had been taken off but now I wanted him, all of him, inside me so I could do it all over again. Nothing else mattered.

"I want to ride you," I gasped, lifting myself off his lap to pull my yoga pants down. My fingers fumbled with the button on his jeans and he lifted his hips enough to let me slide them down. His cock bobbed free and I wrapped my fingers around the hard hot length. Air hissed out between his teeth when I stroked up and down slowly. His hands returned to my hips and his fingers dug into the flesh there as he guided me forward. I climbed over him, straddled his thighs and held his cock upright, enough so that I could rub the head along my slick pussy.

My legs trembled and I sucked in a breath when I moved him over my clit.

"I can feel how wet you are, and I know how good it's going to be when you sink down over me. Fuck Sarah, you're making me crazy." The grip on my hips tightened.

I barely held myself up, teasing his cock with my wetness, working myself up faster than I would have ever imagined. The ridges along his swollen length dragged over my clit and I rocked me hips again. Already I could feel an orgasm building.

Matthew slid his hands up and palmed my breasts, pulled both nipples between his fingers and squeezed them hard. A low groan pulled from my chest and I hovered on the edge, knowing that I was about to fall over it.

With one last drag across my clit that left me teetering on the brink, I angled my hips and sank down over his cock hard, sheathing him in one quick motion. Light exploded behind my eyes and his name ripped from my throat.

Matthew grabbed my hips and drove upward as I clenched around him. "Fuck," he ground out. "Fuck. Fuck."

His breathing grew harsher and his face was all hard lines and tense muscles. dropped my hands to his shoulders and bucked on him. Fissures of pleasure burst through my body and holy hell; I could feel it building again. I couldn't help but whimper.

Ground herself onto him and rocked my hips faster.

"Oh god, Matthew," I panted.

"Don't stop, please." He pulled me against his chest, anchoring me on top of him as he kept thrusting upward. I buried my mouth in his neck, sucked and bit and kissed. Matthew surged, growling low in his throat, and kept up the relentless rhythm. Pressure built inside me. I dragged my lips up over his hard jaw until I found his mouth.

Matthew drove his fingers into my hair, tightened them and held my head still. He kept me there, his eyes devouring me and sank into the dark depths.

Need spiralled faster and faster until I was once again poised on the brink. "Matthew." His name broke free from my lips and his eyes went almost black. "Sarah," he growled, and the sound sank down into my bones. The tension inside me broke free and arched back, clenching around his cock as it throbbed, pulsed inside me.

*****

I stared at the plastic stick in my hand in shock, not sure whether I should laugh or cry at the news I'd just been delivered. Or maybe do both at the same time. That's how conflicted she felt about the entire situation. I was three weeks past due on my period. While I blamed overall stress of the cancer scare, I was never late, and it had taken me this long to gather up the courage to confirm what I already knew in her heart and face the changes already happening with her body.

I went off the pill when my first husband had gotten a vasectomy, but thought after all my body had been through that getting pregnant was something, I didn't think was even feasible. Until this morning.

I swallowed hard, knowing that there wasn't really a decision to be made when I thought of it that way.

I wanted to ask Matthew more questions, to ask why he was so tight lipped about Eden. I wanted to know if only having me was enough. I wanted to reach out and take his hand, or even better: to fold myself into his arms and cling to him.

But things were too strained between Matthew and me. There was a wall between us now, dividing us. A giant elephant in the room: the fight that we'd had the other day, which apparently neither of us was ready to apologise for. And a secret as well.

I rested a hand against my stomach for a brief moment and then retracted it, hoping that he hadn't seen and that he hadn't guessed what the subconscious train of thought was that had led to that motion. I needed to tell him about the baby, but now didn't seem like the right time.

Actually, there were two secrets between us, but the other secret, I wasn't fully ready to admit even to myself. Maybe he wasn't the man I thought I'd married. Either way I had to tell him.

Married Games

Chapter 14

Matthew

She finally pushed through the main door and walked inside. She stopped to glance around to find me, giving me a few precious seconds to take in how beautiful she looked in a pale blue blousy top and a pair of black capri pants.

When her gaze turned in my direction, I lifted my hand to get her attention. I watched her take a deep breath before heading my way, and as she neared, I couldn't help but think how fragile and vulnerable she looked. And very tired.

There was no easy, welcoming smile on her lips. Her eyes lacked their usual vibrancy, and her complexion looked paler than normal. There was no indication that she was happy or excited to see me. No, if anything, her expression reflected a sense of dread.

Yes, she looked as miserable as I felt, but it was the apprehension in the way she approached his table that indicated she wasn't here to confess how much she loved him and it didn't matter about my past. She slid into the chair across from me and gave me a forced smile.

"Hey."

"Hey baby," I replied, and because there was no missing the awkward tension between them, I sought to put her at ease.

"Can I get you something to eat or drink?"

"No, thanks." Her voice was too damned polite, and she looked everywhere but at me.

"This won't take long; I don't want to keep you from your work." I couldn't begin to imagine what she'd come here to tell him, but the fact that she looked so distraught and couldn't even look me in the eyes caused me great concern.

Instinct had me reaching across the table and settling my hand on top of hers. "Sarah... Talk to me please. It's killing me to have you not talk to me?" "I..." She visibly swallowed and finally meeting my gaze, unable to hide the anguish shimmering in the depths.

"I'm pregnant."

I blinked at her, shock rendering me mute. It was the last thing I'd expected to hear, and it took my brain a few extra seconds to process her words.

"You're pregnant?" I echoed dumbly as I gradually pulled my hand away from hers.

"How…" my voice trailed off, severing the stupid question of how did that happen? I knew exactly how it happened; I had fucked her every way possible since the day she'd collected the car from Eden.

I dropped my tone low to keep the conversation private, "I didn't think we, I mean you could have any more children." God the moment the words left my mouth, I felt like a prick.

"Well, apparently the doctors were

wrong. I took a home pregnancy test first a few days ago, then went to my doctor yesterday to confirm the pregnancy before I said anything to you," she said, wringing her hands nervously together. "I'm about five weeks along."

I slumped back in my chair and stared at her, not knowing what to say. So many thoughts and feelings were flying through my head. Stunned disbelief. A spark of panic. And overwhelming fear, because that the reason she had brought me here to tell me she was leaving me.

I couldn't keep up with everything she was saying. I hadn't had time to digest the information as she had, and my head was spinning as I tried to come up with some kind of response.

Sarah abruptly grabbed her purse and stood up, nearly knocking down her chair in the process.

"I need to go."

"Wait." I jumped to my feet just as quickly, my heart hammering in my chest because I wasn't ready for her to go. I stepped toward her. "Sarah—"

They needed to talk… but where did I start when he still hadn't fully accepted or processed that Sarah was pregnant.

"I love you"

Her eyes wide and swimming with tears, she took a meaningful step back.

"I know," she said, her voice tight. She turned around and hurried out of the café without giving me a chance to reply.

Chapter 15

Sarah

The tears began to fall as I left the
cafe. I walked aimlessly through
Federation Square. I couldn't go
home, not yet anyway. I'm not sure
how long I had been wandering

around before a voice pulled me back into reality.

"Sarah is everything okay?" Jeanette's voice full of worry.

But I could stop the tears the moment she spoke.

"Oh, sweetheart, don't cry. I'm sure whatever it is it will work out." Since when did Jeanette care about me. She led me to a park bench urging me to sit.

"Sarah, I know we're not close, but you can talk to me. I understand what it's like to feel alone." Jeanette empathy resonated. It was exactly how I felt. Alone.

*****

It had been a few hours since I had met Matthew in the cafe, and nothing had managed to change my mind that Matthew hadn't wanted the baby.

Even after talking things out with Jeanette I still wasn't convinced. She had to have faith that the world would sort things out, whatever she meant by that. She was a strange woman. When I finally arrived home, Matthew had been waiting in the kitchen.

"Where have you been?" His tone abrupt.

"What the hell do you care, it's not like you want the baby"

"I never said that" his voice low.

"You didn't have to Matthew, your reaction told me everything"

"It was surprised that's all"

I stared at him. "How can you do this?" I cried.

"Do what?" he asked.

"You've taken what should have been a beautiful, happy moment for us and completely ruined it!"

He put his hands on his hips. "Just because I'm not dancing around the house, doesn't mean I'm unhappy."

"Stop lying to me." I pointed at him.

"If you don't want to have a baby with me—"

"I never said that," he roared.

"Stop telling me how I feel, Sarah."

"Well explain it, then Matthew," I replied, not willing to back down.

"I'm fucking scared, okay? I'm scared that I'm going to screw this baby up. I'm not fit to be a Dad. My own father is in prison, in case you haven't noticed."

I stood there, looking into Matthew's pained eyes and knowing immediately that he was telling her the truth.

"Oh, Matthew," she sighed. "You don't have to be scared."

"I don't exactly have a great role model to work off," Matthew said, walking to the bed and sitting on it. He put his palms flat on the bed and bowed his head.

"My childhood was… something no child should ever go through. My adult years were full of bad choices. Up until I met you, that is." He glanced at me and gave a little smile. I crossed over to the bed and sat down next to him.

"You're a good man, Matthew. A really good and kind man and I believe in you completely."

Matthew looked at me and his eyes shown with unshed tears. "I don't want to ever hurt our baby," he said softly.

"Our baby is going to have hard times and struggles just like any other person has. We can't stop that from happening. All we can do is love him.

Or her." Matthew nodded again.

"I love him or her already," he whispered.

Chapter 16

Matthew

After the cluster fuck that had been the revelation that I was going to be a father I had decided it was going to be a night that I indulged my wife in every way possible. What better way than a night of romance, foot massages and sex.

I hadn't realised that changes in her body had already begun. Her breasts had become more sensitive and by god she craved sex. It had been a week since the news of the baby, and I would swear the wife had turned into the most wanton creature ever. So much so that I was retrieving my kit from the club that had been in storage.

I hadn't been back to Highclere in almost two and half years but I knew that all the things I wanted for tonight would still be in the well-maintained condition thanks to a phone call earlier to my longtime friend Jackson resident dom.

As I opened the side entry door of the club a familiar voice echoed through. "She certainly is a sub, her innocence is something I haven't seen in years. Her pussy a ripe little peach just waiting to be picked. I can't wait t get my hands-on Sarah again."

I shook my head. Tell me it's not Eden. It would be too much of a coincidence. I know he joked with me about how much he would love to share her like we did with many other submissive over the years but fuck not Sarah. I could never share her.

I had gone to the club to get my kit bag from the locker when I saw Eden at the bar. It was unlike him to be at the club this early unless he was training a new sub. It looked like he had been there a while, beer in hand and laughing at the conversation he was having with Jackson.

Suddenly Jackson stopped cleaning the glass in front of him and stood over bar across from Eden. "Eden, I know you have mater rights here but I'm warning you now, you mess with another masters sub there are consequences. Matthew won't take this lightly. It's not like the old days when he shared subs. He loves this one. Fuck, he married her for god's sake."

I no longer heard the reply from

Eden. They didn't know I was there and I wasn't about to expose my location. I didn't need to hear anymore. I had to get out of there and now. I threw my kit back into my locker and headed for the car.

I felt hollow as drove back to my office. How could she. My stomach churned as I replayed the conversation I overheard again and again. "Jacko mate, that was the sweetest pussy I have ever had, and fuck did she scream like a whore."

I had only been in my office a few minutes when my intercom buzzed, just as the door to my office opened.

"Your wife, Mr Davidson" my assistants voice rang through.

I couldn't deal with this now, my head was all over the place. The woman I love just crushed my heart. What's worse was I could possibly have been more forgiving it had been anyone else but Eden. Eden had shared subs with me for years before I had met Sarah, but it always went the same way. The sub no longer wanted to have two doms and to be shared. Eden always got the sub. The fucker. That's why I had stepped away from the club and my so-called friend. It was only when I bought new cars or were going to the footy that I had even bother to contact him. It hadn't been the same for years. Not since I'd met Sarah.

"Matthew, we need to talk about the baby" I felt as though the floor had dropped out from under me as the words left her mouth. Anger took root deep in my gut.

"There is no way that baby is mine, if you are really pregnant" I snarled.

"What are you talking about?" Sarah asked, and I almost believed that she was truly confused.

Chapter 17

Sarah

"Matthew, I never slept with Eden," I insisted. "I'm telling you, you're the only man that I slept with."

"Take your lies somewhere else," Matthew said angrily.

"I've had about enough of them! I heard him at the club. He was talking to Jackson, the bartender, telling him all about how he fucked you. How hot and tight your pussy is. I think the details were that first you rode him, and then he pounded into you and how he had you screaming like a whore? Does that sound accurate?"

I felt faint. Whore. That's what he thinks of me. I couldn't believe that Eden had said something like that. From what I knew of the man, even if we had slept together, he wasn't the type to go blabbing the details. But the truth was, we hadn't slept together, so that made it even more puzzling. I didn't know what he was trying to gain by lying about it. I swallowed hard.

"Matthew," I pleaded, taking a step closer, reaching out toward him. But Matthew stepped back, his eyes hard and his arms folded across his broad chest.

"Don't," he said warningly.

Matthew's office intercom buzzed. "Mr Davidson, the coffee you requested is here. I had them get one for your wife also, shall I bring them in, or they will go cold" Fuck, his assistant always had bad timing.

"Bring them in Jeannette" he snapped. God this is her fault, she's just your assistant.

The door of Matthew's office

opened seconds later and the click of Jeannette's heels across the floor broke the silence between Matthew and I, as Jeannette placed the coffees on his desk.

"Is there anything else I can do for you Mr Davidson?" her voice sweet and high like nails on a chalkboard.

"No thank you Jeanette, that will be all for the day. Take the rest of the day off."

"Oh, thank you Sir. Let me know if you need me at all later. I am always available for you, Sir." Janette turned leaving as quickly as she came.

I picked up my coffee and nursed it like it was a shield to protect me from Matthew's anger. Not that it could realistically protect me from anything but I would do anything at that stage to create some distance.

He huffed out another breath. "I don't know what you think you're gaining by lying to me, but I'm not falling for it. He had all the details, Sarah, right down to that scar on your inner thigh. How else would he have known about that, if he didn't see you naked?"

"I have no idea how he knows," I said, shaking my head. "Matthew, I swear to you, I didn't sleep with him. Please."

"What am I supposed to believe Sarah, you tell me you're pregnant and then I hear Eden spooking about how hard he fucked you." Matthew's body shook with anger as he repeatedly ran his hands through his tousled hair.

"I have never been unfaithful to you, I love you, I couldn't " my voice wavering.

"Fuck Sarah, we haven't used protection in years and now suddenly you are pregnant, and I overhear that shit," he growled through his teeth before returning to his seat.

"Matthew, I"

"Just leave Sarah"

I felt like I might burst into tears at any second. I had finally gotten up the courage to tell Matthew about the pregnancy, and now, I was regretting having done so. From the sound of things, he wanted no part in this baby's life. It was enough to have me considering giving the baby up for adoption. I wasn't sure that I could be the mother that I needed to be, knowing that the baby had been born out of such an unhappy relationship. But I knew I couldn't do that.

Chapter 18

Matthew

God, I felt like a prick. I lied to her about the scar. Nothing was said about her scar, but I couldn't help it. I was so angry. So hurt. I watched her leave with tears welling in her eyes, knowing I lied to her. I knew I couldn't go home to our bed tonight; I'd stay in the guest room. I couldn't face Sarah yet. I needed to apologise. God, I need to beg.

I woke the next morning and my hadn't slept hadn't be worth shit. At somewhere between misery and dawn, I decided to go for a run, hoping to clear my head. To get rid of the memory of the hurt I'd seen on her face.

The misery in her eyes gnawed me the entire five kilometres, which completely nullified any good the physical activity might have done. I deserved it though. Deserved every painful step, every sickening punch to the gut that the memories brought.

What kind of husband would say something like that to a wife he cared about? A total bastard, that was who.

Part of me thought that maybe I'd been driven by fear. Eden had gotten under my skin, made me nervous, so much that my mouth had run away with itself.

I didn't know how to handle anything about Sarah and the baby. Even the gut-wrenching need between us that should have been easy, wasn't. There was nothing more fundamental than sex, but what we had wasn't sex .

It was…everything. Sarah was my

everything.

I'd gone and screwed it all up–
again.

I came back from my run even more exhausted than I should have been, completely drained to the bone, an emotional wreck. After a quick shower, I collapsed face-down on my bed and sent Jeanette my secretary a text, telling her I'd be in late.

Being the professional as she was, she didn't ask questions. I had no idea what my schedule was like this morning–she hadn't updated me with meeting notes or anything important, so I had to assume there was nothing major, but things would be shuffled around regardless.

I needed sleep. I also needed to quit thinking about Eden. I no longer cared if I'm not the father of Sarah's baby. I love her too much to lose her.

Chapter 19

Sarah

Something wasn't right. I ran to the toilet once again before lifting the lid and vomiting. I never got morning sickness. I had already had three children in her previous marriage and not one day of morning sickness. That had been a long time ago now but surely my body hadn't changed that much. Another cramping feeling to the stomach and I vomited again.

"Sarah" I heard Matthew call but I couldn't answer. I couldn't move from the cold bathroom tiles that lay cold beneath me.

"Sarah, I know your home. Your keys are on the… Oh fuck" Matthew's feet came into view.

"Sarah, fuck." Matthew pushed my hair aside and lowered his head to what I can only assume was listening for my breathing.

"Sarah, talk to me, what

happened" his voice full urgency.

I tried to speak but nothing came out. My whole body felt like I was asleep.

"Hello, emergency. My wife has collapsed in the bathroom." The panic in Matthews' voice clear.

My baby, please not my baby. The baby has to be ok. Please god, don't take my baby.

*****

Dark, light, dark, light. I could feel the rush of air as they pushed me through the emergency room doors.

"Thirty-six year old female, collapsed on the floor of her home.

Her husband tells us she's five weeks pregnant."

"She's haemorrhaging." Darkness consumed me again.

*****

My eyes were starting to adjust to the light, and Matthew was coming into focus, his face sharpening, the look in his eyes intensifying and becoming more clear, like puzzle pieces shifting into place.

"Matthew ," I whispered, because I wanted to tell him how I felt, wanted to tell him I was sorry, sorry I had lost our baby.

"Shhh. It's okay, baby," he murmured. "Shh. It's okay."

I nodded, the tears welling in my eyes. His index finger grazed my lips, and he rested his palm on my cheek, brushing his thumb under my eye, wiping my tears.

The curtain of the emergency room cubical opened.

"Ah, your awake, I will just go and get the doctor." The nurse scurried off returning a few minutes later with an older man in green scrubs that looked like he had a long shift.

"Mrs Davidson, as you are aware you miscarried tonight and to be honest, I am a little confused as your blood results came back. I'm afraid we have found something rather disturbing. Have you ever heard of the drug Mifepristone" the doctor flipped through my chart.

"No, should I have?"

"It's an abortion drug. It is taken by mouth and ends a pregnancy by blocking the action of the hormone (progesterone) that supports the pregnancy. Would there be a reason why you would take that drug, without seeking medical help?"

I inhaled, a sharp intake of breath that I held in my lungs, not trusting myself to speak without screaming. The air burned my chest as I held it as long as I could, until my head started to feel slightly woozy and I was forced to blow it slowly out of my nose. Matthew didn't say anything. I turned and looked away, biting back my tears.

"I would never harm my baby" I said through gritted teeth.

Fury rose in my chest and my free hand curled into a fist by my side, the sharp bite of my fingernails digging into my palms. How could they think I would do this.

"Mr Davidson, is there any reason you would want to harm yourself? This the third trip to the hospital you've made in only a matter of months. If you hadn't wanted to have this baby there are more appropriate ways it can be dealt with," the doctor peered over the chart with at me. How dare he. I would never.

Chapter 20

Matthew

"No that can't be right my wife wanted this baby, we both did." Matthew refuted. It can't be true; Sarah would never do that. Sarah could never take a life it just wasn't in her to do that.

"Mr Davidson, can you please take a seat outside while I speak with your wife," the doctor turned to me before pointing towards the waiting room.

" I will not be going anywhere, anything you have to say to my wife, I will be here for."

It was then that two Victorian police officers entered the emergency ward cubicle. What the hell is going on.

"Mr Davidson, if you please." The officer pointed in the direction of the waiting room.

The officer lead into the emergency room hallway. "Mr

Davidson, we would like to ask you some questions about your wife. Would she have any reason to harm herself or your unborn child?"

My anger grew this bastard didn't give a shit. My wife just lost our baby. God, was it mine? Or was it Eden's. Fuck, I couldn't tell the police that. It didn't matter right now. All that mattered is that Sarah would be ok.

"Look officer, when I left for work this morning my wife had said she was feeling off like she was getting a bug of some sort, you know the usual. Nausea, diarrhoea, dizziness, headache and fever."

I knew I was lying but I can't imagine Sarah wanting to harm herself let alone her unborn baby.

The officer shook his head. "Mr Davidson, I understand that this may be difficult time for you but this sort of thing doesn't happen every day. Somethings not right with this."

"You're fucking right there. How dare you accuse my wife of doing this to herself. If you have nothing more, I would like to get back to her and take her out of this hellhole." It was then I noticed that everyone had stopped to stare at us. I knew I shouldn't have sworn at the officer but I too angry not to react.

"That is all for now Mr Davidson, I will excuse your behaviour for now due to the circumstances but do not ever speak like that to me again. You are free to go."

*****

I kept glancing over at Sarah on the ride home, but she didn't dissolve into tears again. Instead, she stared numbly out the window, her eyes barely registering anything. I knew she was exhausted after that bout of crying, but I couldn't help feeling worried about her, wishing that she would show a little more life.

She was nothing more than a shell. I helped her up the elevator to our penthouse apartment and through to our bedroom. She hadn't spoken a word the whole way up.

I sighed, pulling the back the bed covers so that she could slid beneath. I didn't know what to say. I walked down the hall to the kitchen, returning with a glass of water placing on the bedside. Sarah had already turned away and drifted off to sleep.

Outside in the hallway, I leaned against the wall, closing my eyes and counting to ten. I hated to see her like this, in so much pain. I only wished that this hadn't happened to her. But I couldn't think about all of the 'what ifs' and 'could haves' now.

I watched through the open bedroom door; her light hair was a tangle on the pillow. Her lips parted as she slept. I couldn't resist anymore. I needed to feel her close to me. Stripping down as I walked into our bedroom, I climbed carefully into the bed and pulled her into my arms. Every tear felt like a knife to my heart as I pondered everything that had happened, wondering if this was all my fault.

I sighed, and for a moment, I tightened my arms around Sarah, who shifted in her sleep as though she could sense my distress. I quickly relaxed my arms, holding my breath and hoping that she kept sleeping. Fortunately, she did.

Chapter 21

Sarah

It had been three weeks since my miscarriage and nothing had been the same. Matthew had worked late almost every day and even when he did arrive home, conversations were limited to basic pleasantries. To make matters worse he'd slept in the spare room every night. It was clear he didn't believe that the lost baby hadn't been his or maybe he thought I was callous enough to kill my unborn child. Either way he hadn't wanted to be with me.

Was this the beginning of the end for our marriage?

I called Matthew and hung up as fear that our marriage might be finished over. The moment I placed my phone back on the desk it started to ring.

I didn't allow myself time to actually think about the action. I just answered it.

"Hello."

"Please don't hang up." The pleading note in his voice tugged at my heart.

"I'm listening," I said softly.

"I know you this is chicken of me but I can't hold back anymore. These past few weeks have been hell. I can't sleep or concentrate. I think about you all the time, Sarah." The words came pouring out of him in a rush, and they could've been my words, my feelings.

"It's killing me not being with you, Sarah." He fell silent for a moment, as if waiting for me to tell him to leave me alone, to hang up, to do something.

"Is that why you called?" I asked. My heart hammered against my ribcage as I waited for his answer.

"Yes." He kept it simple, and that one word thrilled me. "You have no idea what being away from you is doing to me. I love you Sarah."

I thought about how little I'd accomplished, and almost said that I had a pretty good idea.

"Every time I close my eyes, all I can see is you. Your eyes. Your smile. Your body." His voice held a pleading note.

"I need you."

I swallowed hard. How could I say no to that?

Chapter 22

Matthew

I stood by the elevator of my office waiting to go home. What a day. Sarah and I finally spoke. It may have

been on the phone but it was a start.
Now it was time to go home and sink
myself into my wife but I was
stopped in my tracks when I reached
the building underground car park.
Eden stood by my vehicle. What the
fuck did he want now.

"Get out of the way Eden" I didn't
want to deal with this right now.
Sarah was at home waiting for me.

"Poor Matthew, did you have a
bad day?"

"Fuck off Eden, I think you have
done enough" I grunted before
reaching for my car door.

"I think you should listen
Matthew, I think you will be very
interested in what I have to say.

Especially about your little whore"
his voice dripping with sarcasm that I
wanted to beat out of him.

"What did you call her" I turned
rage flowing through my veins.

"You know what happens when
you don't share your toys Matthew?
They get broken in the fight for
them." Eden flicked of what seemed
to be an invisible piece of lint from
the breast of his tailored jacket.

"What the fuck are you talking
about Eden" my voice betraying the
control I wanted but couldn't reach.

"I'm talking about you keeping me
away from what should be mine, we
share remember. We made a promise
to each other years ago that we

shared. Everything. And if you don't want to share... Well I will just take you little toy away because you've been a bad boy. We wouldn't want Sarah to know all your secrets, now would we?"

My head spun. What the game was he playing at. Sarah is my wife not some game.

"What do you want Eden?" my face heating with rage, if this didn't end quickly, I may just kill the bastard.

"I want what I always want Matthew, what's yours and you." His voice so matter of fact that was if he expected me to already know the answer.

I lurched forward and grabbed my so-called friend by the collar of his shirt and slammed him against the car.

"Keep your fucking hands off Sarah, if you touch her again"

Eden laughed, why the fuck was he laughing.

"You think I fucked your precious little sub already" the laughter continued in his voice. "I didn't fuck her. Oh no no no, that's something we do together remember. I did help get rid of that little problem though. I couldn't have something like that come between us. I only share with you Matthew and no pitter patter of little feet will stop me from getting what I want."

I swallowed hard, not even wanting to consider the truth of that last part of his statement. He'd made Sarah miscarry. My child. He'd played me. He knew somehow that I would be there and hear him. He knew what I'd do. I hadn't believed her.

I dropped my hand and stepped back feeling as like all the breath had been kicked out of me.

"Ah, the penny drops"

"What the fuck did you do to her" I rushed at my ex-friend not hesitating to hit him this time. He was ready this time. He wrestled out of the way just as my fist hit the drivers window shatter it. I stepped back my hand marred with blood. Eden stood before me pistol in hand.

"Now, now. Play nice Matthew, you don't want poor little Sarah to have more health problems do you," A sly grin on his face.

"What the do you want Eden?" I ground out.

"Well, Matthew I just want you to be a good boy. So, when I tell you, you are going to get into your car and you're going to go home and tell that fuckable little sub of yours nothing. If you do anything to deviate from my plan, the loss of your unborn child will look like child's play." Eden laughed again and shrugged his shoulders. "Too soon"

I had no choice, I had to walk away. If he was able to force my wife to have a miscarriage, then he wouldn't think twice on using the gun on me. I got in my car, drove away watching Eden in the review mirror as I left.

I cursed myself. Sarah.

I'd gotten her involved. But it went beyond my believing that she had slept with someone else; I hadn't supported her when she'd told me that she was pregnant, either. Instead, I'd accused her of being pregnant with another man's child. I felt sick, just thinking about the emotional turmoil she had been going through.

My job, above everything else, was to protect her. It was to keep her safe. And I was failing.

"My God," I said to myself, and my head as banged my hand against the steering wheel. I bit back the scream that threatened to erupt from my throat. "My God, Matthew, what have you done?"

Chapter 23

Sarah

Matthew had been extremely possessive over the past week. He'd spent every opportunity at home and he'd spent even more time inside of me. It was if he'd been making up for lost time. He'd started talking to me about his childhood years and slowly he had started opening up about his year at Highclere.

Last night he had introduced me to handcuffs. The feeling on hard metal against my wrists. I still wore the faint red line around my wrist this morning. I hadn't bothered covering them as it was a reminder of Matthew. The Matthew, I was only just getting to know.

I had go with him to the office this morning before I was heading off for a book signing at a local book store. We had barely made it to Matthew's floor before he'd started touching me in the elevator.

"Mrs Davidson," he said. "You are looking more beautiful than ever."

"Why thank you, Mr Davidson."

He pulled me to him and kissed me, and I flushed. He unbuttoned the top of my shirt, just a couple of buttons, inspecting the top of my breasts. "You have the most fantastic breast, Mrs Davidson."

He tipped my chin up and kissed me, his tongue rubbing against mine, his stubble raking across my cheeks, his hands roaming my body. He kissed me until I was breathless, senseless, dizzy. It was when backside hit something had that I realised he'd maneuvered us into the conference room.

There was a sound from out in the hallway the ding of the elevator. Jeanette had arrived. Matthew gave me a cocky grin as his hands continued roaming over my ass, apparently not caring that we could be caught. "Matthew," I protested, grabbing at his hand, but his hands continued roaming over my skin, pushing my skirt up.

I could hear the sound of Jeanette's heels clicking against the floor as they came closer. I blushed hot at the thought of her catching me with my skirt up. But Matthew managed to pull it down just as the door to the conference room opened. He was still holding me close, his hand now on my waist, my chest flush with his.

"Oh," Jeanette said when she saw us. Her face, as always, was flawless, her skin poreless and perfect, her hair pulled back in a low bun. She was wearing a grey shift dress and pearls, and she was somehow able to look professional and sexy at the same time.

My blouse and skirt, which had up until a moment ago seemed fine, suddenly felt like I was a kid trying to play dress up.

"I'm sorry, I didn't–"

"It's fine," Matthew said.

"Come in, come in." He kissed me softly on the lips before letting me go, and I blushed at his public display of affection. Jeanette's eyes met mine, and I saw the look of annoyance that flashed there. Her eyes slid down to my open blouse. I followed her gaze to where my top two buttons were undone, and you could see the top of the lace bra Matthew had bought me last week. But not all of it, thank God.

I quickly did the two buttons and pulled at my sleeves, making sure my wrists were covered as they still don the marks from last night. Jeanette gave me look of disgust and I blushed. Matthew kissed me lightly before turning to address Jeanette more directly which I took as my cue to leave before things became more awkward.

Chapter 24

Matthew

Sarah had finally gotten back into her routine of writing after the last couple of months of turmoil. I watched through the doorway as she sat at her computer, headphones on, listening to whatever god-awful country music that was bound to be playing. It was usually one of her favourites like Garth Brooks or Keith Urban. She was a sucker for a romantic cowboy. She must have been, she had written over fifteen romance novels about them and the big alpha males that always win the girl. It made me wonder was this our love story. Did I get to keep the girl in the end? I shook my head; I couldn't leave it to chance that I got her in the end.

It had been a typical Saturday night. In fact, it was the first Saturday night in months that we had decided to stay in. I need to get back to the way things used to be and what better than have a few wines and a nice cheese platter.

We started with a bottle of crisp white Sauvignon Blanc and Sarah had barely finished her first glass of Shiraz. Cheese and wine had always been our thing. The cheese platter had had all of my favourites, a beautiful Tasmanian blue, a creamy triple Brie and apricot and almond cheese, topped off with Sarah's favourite Danish salami and line of plain and peppered crackers on each side of the board. We even had our favourite YouTube playlist running on the television in the lounge room as background noise.

Sarah suddenly jumped from the couch and ran towards the bathroom.

"Baby, are you ok?" I called through the bathroom door. The vomiting noise continued before a flush of the toilet.

"Sarah" but there was no answer. I waited as we weren't the type of couple to share our toileting moments with each other. I passed back down the hall and too the rubbish bin pulling the cheese wrappers to check the used by dates. Made be its the cheese and I hadn't noticed. Nope. All still in date.

We had eaten and drunk the same things so it couldn't be the wine. I poured myself another glass of red.

I heard Sarah's footsteps before I saw here.

"Did you drug me?" Her finger point and her face pink in anger.

"What, how could you…" I didn't even have a chance to reply before the banging on the front door began.

"Police open up "voices flowed through our penthouse apartment.

"Sarah, what the fuck" I turned walking to open the door and sort out what seems to be a huge misunderstanding. Just as I open the door, I hear a thud behind me. Shit. Sarah had collapsed to the floor.

Four police streamed in on rushing to Sarah and another shoving me hard against the wall. As he held me in place, I could only watch in horror at my wife unconscious on the lounge room floor.

"Let me go" I begged as paramedics entered.

"The only place you are going Mr Davidson is with us" The officer pushed me against me cuffing my hands behind my back.

"Fuck. Let me go" I yelled struggling against the cuffs. "You have to let me go with my wife"

Chapter 25

Sarah

My head began to pound. The blood rushed through my body, faster and faster, becoming more intense with each beat of my heart. My veins expanded and pulsed, and my temples throbbed. The panic rolled in like a tide, threatening to overtake me, and I forced my mind to move faster in an attempt to stay ahead of it. I felt completely disconnected from my body, like what was happening to me wasn't real.

I ran to the bathroom and vomited. Really, again. Last time I had been vomiting was the day I miscarried. I knew this time there was no chance that I was pregnant, so maybe it's the cheese? It can't be the wine we hadn't drunk that much. I vomited again hearing Matthew checking on me through the closed door. As stood to wash my hands my phone buzzed in my pocket.

Enjoying your night? - number unknown

What the hell, was someone messing with me? My fingers flew across my phone screen in reply.

Who is this? - Sarah Davidson

Your husband isn't everything you thought he was, is he?
Want to know why your sick tonight? Ask your husband.
- number unknown

I don't know what sick joke you

**are playing but leave us alone -
Sarah**

**Oh Sarah, I'm only getting just
getting started - number unknown**

I turned stalking back to the
lounge room when another bout of
nausea rose in my throat and
dizziness plagued me. I spoke but
made no sense of the words coming
out of my mouth. A pounding
banging as if my head was inside of
drum began. Everything went black.

"Ma'am, can you hear us" voices
broke through the darkness. I tried to
respond but the words wouldn't
come out.

"Ma'am. Do you know where you are?" the voice said again.

My head lolled from side to side.

"Let me go" my husbands voice made me still. I tried to focus my eyes to where his voice was coming from. As I turned my head a police officer was pushing against my husband who was now cuffed against the wall.

"NO"

"Ma'am please you need to remain calm." The paramedic above me finally came into focus.

Matthew continued to fight against his cuffs before another officer joined then and dragged them out the front door. The Victorian police had taken Matthew away. Taken him away from our inner-city penthouse apartment in handcuffs, like a common criminal. He's been arrested.

"No. I need to get up. Please, I need my husband."

Why were they taking my husband. I tried to swing my legs over the side of the stretcher and to hop down but the paramedic put his hands on my shoulders and gently pushed me back down.

Before I knew what, I was doing, before I could even think about it, I bit him on the arm. A second later, as if out of nowhere, a team of people surrounded me. Police and paramedics.

"Get me two of lorazapam,"

someone said. I felt them inject me with something, the sharpness of the needle biting into my arm.

"No," I said.

"No, please! Stop!" I kicked and screamed, but they didn't listen.

I'm one of those crazy people, I thought, stunned. I'm one of those crazy insane people who needs to be knocked out because they can't be trusted not to hurt someone. It was the last thought I remember having before everything went dark.

*****

There were only flashes after that. A nurse placing a blood pressure cuff around my arm. The prick of an IV. The cool feel of a stethoscope against my neck.

Gradually, everything began fading back in, until I was able to open my eyes and take in my surroundings. I was in a hospital room, and a nurse stood at the side of my bed, checking one of my monitors. She looked over at me, her eyes bright.

"You're awake," she said, sounding pleased.

"Yes." I swallowed and tried to keep myself as calm as possible. The last thing I wanted was to get drugged again.

"Where's my husband?"

"Who?" the nurse asked, her face wrinkling in confusion.

"My husband, Matthew," she chewed her lip.

"I'll go get the doctor," she said. The doctor appeared a few moments later and introduced herself as Dr. Mackenzie. She was tall with her dark shiny hair pinned to the top of her head and what looked to be an undercut underneath.

"How are you feeling, Sarah?" she asked.

"Groggy."

She nodded. "That's from the sedative we gave you. It should be wearing off soon." She grabbed my chart and scanned it. "Do you remember anything from last night?"

"No, where is my husband" my frustration showing

"He was arrested," her voice solemn as if to say she'd seen it all before.

"Arrested ?" I asked through my tears. She sighed.

"Sarah–"

"Please," I said. "Please, I …I need to leave."

She bit her lip, then nodded and gave me a smile.

"Okay, but you have to take it easy. But you have to promise that you won't operate a vehicle."

I shook my head. "I won't."

The taxi took me to the police

station, and I walked towards the front entrance, trying not to be intimidated when seeing all of the police cars parked in the lot. Everything about the place screamed authority, and power and as a whole it made me feel small and powerless.

Somehow, just walking inside, I felt guilty, as if she'd committed a crime and was about to be discovered.

I haven't done anything wrong. I'm not guilty of anything and neither is Matthew.

Are you absolutely sure of that? How well do you really know him?

My mind continued spouting arguments and refutations as I

continued into the station. There were some chairs and benches, and across the room, a window looking into a back office of some sort. The police don't just arrest people for no reason.

Perhaps I really didn't know my husband as well as I thought I did.

My mouth felt dry, and her heart was pounding an unsteady rhythm in my chest as she approached the window, behind which a uniformed female officer sat talking on a landline. I waited fidgeting until the officer got off the phone before approaching.

"Hi," she said, uncertainly. The officer was short and squat, with a flat nose and dull brown eyes. "How can I assist you?"

I took a deep breath. "My husband was arrested and brought to this—

"Name," the woman replied, moving to her computer keyboard.

"My name or—"

"His," she interrupted.

"Oh. Matthew. Matthew Davidson."

There was a clacking of the keyboard as the officer's fingers rattled over the keys in rapid-fire fashion.

"He's in Central Booking," the woman informed her.

"I'm sorry, I don't know what—"

"Central Booking is where people go to wait until they reach bail. Your husband's been arrested, and he'll have to wait like everyone else to see if gets bail." The woman moved away from the computer and picked up a large metal coffee cup. She sipped at it and then started filling out some paperwork, seemingly done with the conversation.

"Ummm… excuse me, ma'am?" I asked softly. The officer didn't turn her head, just kept working. Another person stepped into line behind me and the officer looked up and waved that person forward.

"How can I help you, Sir?" the woman said. I didn't move from the window. "Wait a second, I was here first."

"I answered your question," the woman behind the window said.

"Your husband is awaiting his arraignment. Sometime in the next twenty-four hours, he'll have his time in front of a judge. And if you'll excuse me, I have other people to help."

"That wasn't help," I grumbled my cheeks flushing.

"How dare you treat me like I'm just some annoying little pest? I'm a person, and my husband's been arrested, and I'm frightened."

The officer pursed her lips and took a deep breath.

"Most people who come in here are scared."

"I need to see my husband immediately."

"He's not allowed visitors. If he is released from custody today, he will be out in a few hours."

"So, I can't even see him?"

"I'm not the arresting officer, so I really don't know what else to tell you." The officer waved forward the man standing behind me again.

Chapter 26

Matthew

As I walked myself into the entry of the station, followed by my very tall and expensive lawyer in a grey suit and a police officer who seemed to be escorting us to the door. When I saw Sarah sitting there, my eyes widened.

"What are you doing?" he said.

"I—I came here to find you," she replied, and then burst into tears. It was humiliating. I couldn't help myself as arms were around her, lifting her to her feet and then hugging her tightly to me.

"Shhh… it's okay. Calm down." Sarah was shaking with relief. She grabbed on tightly to my shirt as she pushed her face into my chest.

"I was so scared…. so, so scared."

"Come outside with me," I told her before turning to the man I had no choice but to trust. My lawyer. "I need to get her out of here."

"That's fine. I can take care of the paperwork. I'll meet you in a few hours." I nodded at my lawyer and walked Sarah outside the station and then brought her to a nearby bench and sat down with her.

"How… how did you get out?" she asked. "Did they drop the charges?" Matthew laughed. "Not quite. I'm free on bail."

Sarah took a deep, shuddering breath in and then let it out, collapsing against Matthew, laying her head on my shoulder.

"I'm so relieved. You have no idea. I was just sitting there, waiting for you to call me." I was silent. I rubbed

her back and didn't say anything.
Sarah lifted her head and looked at
me. I knew my eyes were distant. But
I couldn't change how I felt.

"Matthew?" she asked.

I glanced at her. "Yes?"

"They said you were allowed three
calls. Why didn't you use one of them
to call me?"

I made a grunting noise.

"I was a little preoccupied with
trying to get myself out of jail as
quickly as possible. And I knew there
wasn't anything you'd be able to do
to help that happen."

I could see that Sarah felt
wounded.

"I'm your wife. Aren't you

supposed to call your wife?"

I slid away from her and my body tensed.

"Sarah," my voice a hiss of impatience. I lowered my head and ran my hands through my thick hair.

"I really can't do this right now."

"Do what?"

"Sit here and justify everything I did after I got arrested." I sat straight up and turned my head to stare at her. My eyes were burning bright with frustration.

"I was just arrested because someone made an anonymous photo call saying that I drugged and abused my wife."

She looked away from him and

her tears seemed to instantly vanish.

"What," she said. "That wasn't me, Matthew."

Sarah got up and started to walk away from me, shaking her head. I jumped to his feet and caught her, grabbing her wrist.

"Stop. Stop it right now."

Sarah turned to face me.

"What happened last night Matthew?" her voice small like a child asking for something she knew she wasn't allowed to have.

"You that's what happened last night"

"Why are you so cruel to me?" I knew that my face was a mask that she couldn't penetrate.

"I'm tired," I said.

"So am I, Matthew," she said, her voice cracked.

I sighed. "I will talk to my lawyer in a few hours and discuss the charges."

"No, You're going to beat the charges because you're innocent." Her voice more confident then he'd heard in a while.

"What makes you think I'm as innocent as you claim me to be."

"Because Matthew, I know you'd never hurt me. Ever."

Chapter 27

Sarah

We arrived back at home and not spoken much. Matthew had announced his intention to take a long, hot shower, and then disappeared. I sat down and tried to watch some television but found it hard to focus on anything. She kept replaying moments from the last. Remembering the moment, I had woken up in the hospital alone and fuzzy moments the police had stormed into our home when Matthew had been placed in handcuffs and told that he was being arrested.

The truth was I had no idea what had happened in the last twenty-four hours. The only thing I did know was that I am exhausted, but I don't want to close my eyes. Matthew wouldn't have hurt me… He is the most loving, supportive and caring man I have ever met. I know he loves me.

Matthew finally emerged downstairs in sweatpants and a white t-shirt, looking refreshed from his shower. Every time I saw him, I was still struck by how ferociously gorgeous the man was. His dark hair was still damp from the shower, the fringe hanging over his forehead. My gaze moved to his strong jaw, those cobalt blue eyes, and then she took in the tight, toned body that was tantalisingly within reach as he came towards me.

"You look tired," he said.

"I'm am," I admitted.

"Do you want to go to sleep?"

"Sure, if you are ready." My reply

not exactly a question but more of a statement to see if Matthew had planned to sleep next to me in our bed tonight.

As I enter our bedroom Matthew's arms surround me and his mouth hot on my neck. His licks hot lashes sending shivers of pleasure through my body.

Warning bells go off in my head. I need to take control of this situation. I need to get answers not get seduced by my husband. But his tongue brushes against my neck again, and all of my protests slip out of my head. Certainly, there's nothing wrong with teasing him a little, letting him think I've succumbed to his charms. I'll give him a taste, fuel his desire, and then I'll have him right where I want him. He tightens his hold on my hip, pulling me closer to him. His other hand moves to the shoulder of my shirt, yanking it aside so he can continue his soft march of kisses. I shiver involuntarily.

"Matthew," I whisper.

"Perhaps we should—" I gasp as he nips at me with his teeth.

"Is that what you really want?" he says against my skin. His hand moves forward along the neckline of my shirt, his fingers skimming just beneath the edge of the fabric. He slides the garment off my shoulder, exposing the top curve of my breast.

"You have such beautiful breasts Sarah," he says, his mouth against my ear once more. His hand moves lower, gliding over one of my breasts and then the other, his touch featherlight. My breathing is shallow, uneven. I know I should stop him, take back control of the situation, but I don't. In this moment I'm not even sure I want to.

"Feel the frustration building?" he breathes against my ear.

His hand moves lower and lower, with such agonising slowness that I have to struggle to keep from pressing back against him. His fingers graze my nipple. I stiffen as he takes the nub and rolls it gently between his forefinger and thumb.

"It's subtle at first," he whispers, giving a soft pull.

"Your blood pumping faster, your skin becoming more sensitive. The beginning of an ache between your legs." His fingers become more insistent, pinching and tugging at my nipple.

"That's where we want to focus. On that ache." I close my eyes and let my head roll back against his shoulder. My nipple is rock hard beneath his touch, and still he massages it, pulling and twisting to the point of pain. I should tell him to stop, but I don't.

And then, suddenly, his fingers

release me. A sound of protest escapes me before I can stop it, and Matthew chuckles into my hair.

"We're not done yet," he says. He moves to the other breast, pulling it halfway out of the shirt so that he can reach the nipple. He repeats his rolling and pulling until that one, too, is hard and sensitive against his rougher skin. "It builds slowly," he murmurs into my hair.

"But little by the little the ache grows stronger, more insistent."

He moves his hand from my hip and across my upper thigh, stopping at the place where my legs meet. He pushes down softly, just enough to press the fabric of the skirt against my most sensitive spot.

"What, then, is the cause of this frustration?" he breathes.

His hand slides further between my legs. I push back against him involuntarily, and he tightens his grip on me, keeping me hard against him. I know that I need to stop him. I need to pull away. I need to control this situation. I need answers.

"Matthew… Stop" my voice is breathy.

"Oh Sarah, just give me this. Please."

"Matthew, I need…" my words are cut off.

"So wet already," he whispers in my ear. His hand moves slowly—too slowly. I squirm against him.

This is a bad idea, a tiny voice in my head reminds me. Stop him. Push him away. You're supposed to be the one in control. You're supposed to get answers.

With all my strength, I push away from him. I have too.

"Matthew… I can't"

Chapter 28

Matthew

I knew that Sarah wanted answers but I had nothing. I didn't know. All I knew is that right now I needed her. I needed her naked and under me. My frustration grew.

Chapter 29

Sarah

"Dammit, Sarah , don't leave me hanging," he says.

"I'm not leaving you hanging I need to know what the hell happened last night. Where the hell did the police come from and how did I end up in the hospital?" But it's when he reaches for me again that really ticks me off.

"What the fuck is going on? Fuck this! I'm not your fucking puppet! You can't just expect me to have all this shit happen and not as questions."

"Look, Sarah, I'm sorry," Matthew said sounding defeated.

"You just drive me crazy, you know that? Please. Please. I promise answer anything you want just come to bed with me. I need you."

I'm having trouble standing still, so I grab Matthew's shirt from the ground and slip it on. I march over to the table, grab our half-finished bottle of wine from dinner, and head over to the glass sliding doors at the far side of the dining room. I don't care that it's raining. I pull open the doors and step out onto the balcony. We were on the eightieth floor of the Eureka tower in Melbourne.

The cold, wet air is a welcome slap in the face. A welcome relief. The rain has slowed to a drizzle and wind howled around me. I lean against the railing and take a swig of wine right from the bottle.

I didn't care if it wasn't ladylike as my mother would have said. My life is a mess, and I'm not sure what to do anymore. Did Matthew do this, did I? What wasn't he telling me? Could I still trust the man I married? Or was this my doing? Did I get my husband arrested?

I take another swig and stare out across the city lights still visible through the drizzle. How did life get so fucked up.

"Drinking without me?" Matthew's voice snaps me out of my thoughts.

He holds out his hand for the wine bottle, and I pass it over. He takes a drink and hands it back. "Sarah, I would never hurt you. You have to know that. I love you more than my next breath. As for what happened last night…" Matthew sighed. "I have no idea what happened..."

"But you must, it was just us here" I pleaded.

"It was just us, that's what I don't understand. One minute we were enjoying some wine, cheese and music. Then you were in the bathroom vomiting. "

"But we hadn't drunk much" my voice sounding as confused as I felt.

"Exactly, that's what I can't work out. One minute all was fine and the next you accused me of spiking your drink and you were vomiting." Matthew voice was strained like the memories of my accusation had truly hurt him.

"I don't get it, why would I say that." I stepped forward raising my hand to touch Matthew.

"I don't know, but you did." Matthew shrugged.

I stepped forward wrapping my arms around him. "Oh, Matthew. I'm sorry. I'm so sorry. I know you'd never do that to me."

Chapter 30

Matthew

I had been in and out of meetings with investors for a new seventy story project in their city offices when my phone dinged. I swiped the message open. Eden. It had been weeks since the underground car park incident and weeks since his threats about Sarah.

I have a little present for you, it will be just like old times - E

I immediately tried to call Sarah. Fuck, no answer. I dialled again. Still no answer. My heart raced. Why isn't she picking up.

What have you done to her? - M

Why don't you come and see. She ready and waiting like a good girl? - E

Tell me where she is - M

I raced home continuing to call Sarah's phone. As I arrived, I searched apartment. Nothing.

Tell me where the fuck my wife is - M

Oh, Matthew you should know by now I always come to you. We are just catching on lost time. - E

The next thing I received is a video file. That's where I knew this deadly game Eden was playing had to stop and now.

"Matthew, please, please save us" Jeanette's frantic scream on the screen in front of me, sent chills through me. She'd been tied up. She said us. Eden must have Sarah too. Why, Jeanette. She is just my secretary. I replayed the video looking for clues to where they were. The scene panned across Jeanette again. The logo. Shit my logo. My office.

I called triple 000. I knew this wasn't something that was going to turn out well. Not after my last run in with Eden.

I couldn't take any chances. Sarah and Jeanette were in trouble.

"What the hell is going on?" I muttered under my breath as I looked up from the service elevator from the car park and saw nothing. I crossed the marble flooring. The building looked empty. Why wasn't security at the front desk.

Walked down the hall I could hear Eden before I saw him.

"YOU BITCH," he yelled.

Chapter 31

Sarah

I'd come to see if Matthew had wanted to go for lunch after everything we'd been through and then last night. That's when I heard the voices. Yelling coming from his office.

The door was slightly ajar, and I could see Matthew from where I was standing. I recognised the other voice.

Eden.

I cracked the door to intervene. Matthew shook his head letting me know that it wasn't safe. I dial 000 as I shut the door and waited for the police to arrive and stop this madness. As the argument got more heated, I heard the rise and fall of angry voices and then silence. That worried me. I cracked the door and saw Matthew laying face down on the wooden floor as Eden pulled Jeanette off the office chair and positioned her next to Matthew.

"I know you're out there, Sarah!" Eden called from Matthew's office. I quietly closed the door and placed the Jeanette's reception chair under the handle, trying to figure out what to do next.

"Sarah, why don't you come in here an join us. Don't you want to know why Matthew has been such a bad boy?" he yelled.

"Let them go," I called back as I looked around the room for a possible weapon before yelling, "Why Eden, Why are you doing this?"

"Sarah, Sarah, Sarah. Our dear Mathew here just doesn't like to share his new toy."

Shit Eden's talking about me. He wants to share me. God, what do I do? Keep him talking the longer he talks the more likely help will come.

"Why is sharing me, so important to you?"

"Oh sweetheart, I don't merely want to share. I want him. He was always supposed to be mine. But no, a little whore like you caught his eye," he said startling me as he threw himself against the door and shoved it open enough to get the hand holding the gun pointed straight at me.

"I don't have anything to lose anymore, Sarah. You're going to pay for you taking what was mine."

"Eden, none of this makes any sense," I said as I moved toward the corner where he couldn't see me, thinking that if he started shooting at least I'd have some chance of avoiding the bullets.

"It doesn't matter," he growled. "Nothing matters anymore."

"So, you're going to kill us all because Matthew wouldn't have sex with you. Because he wouldn't share?" I asked as I searched for a way to keep him talking. " Why did you come to us, why didn't you just ask."

"Shut the fuck up," Eden growled again. "I deserved to have him, after all the years of playing second fiddle to all the whores and subs he used."

"I'm not his sub, " my voice flat .

"You have no clue do you, he might have come off all sweet and romantic, but he has needs. Needs you will never fill. I could have made him happy but no. You got your claws into him and just had to fix him didn't you," he said as I watched his arm slide down the door frame.

Suddenly, on the other side of the door, I heard a loud bang and then saw Eden pull the gun out of the crack between the door and the frame. I heard a loud thud and then two voices shouting in the hallway. I stayed crouched in the space between the wall and the door frame as the gun went off. I heard another thud, and then a voice broke the silence that followed.

"He's dead, but you going to take his place. You're going to be my little bitch, and do exactly as I say or you'll have a bullet in you just like Matthew," Eden said quietly. His voice sent a chill up my spine.

"Don't do it! Don't do it!" Jeanette screamed from Matthew's office. I knew I had one chance to stop this deadly plan and, that either way, I had a pretty good chance of dying. I decided it was better to have it over with quickly rather than having to suffer.

So, I yanked open the door and ran towards Eden where he stood with a knife in one hand and the gun in the other. I raced toward him with my eye on the gun from his hand.

Halfway there, I heard a loud crack as the frosted glass of office door shattered and Eden slumped to the ground.

Bewildered, I looked around trying to figure out what had just happened. Eden rose up with the gun in his hand and pointed it at me. I screamed as the second shot hit him and he fell over dropping the gun to the floor. I kicked it out of the way and ran to Jeanette who was crying hysterically in a pool of shattered glass. She'd been cut, but as I untied the ropes that bound her.

"He shot him!" she cried as she pointed towards the conference room that back onto Matthews office. I ran around to the doorway and saw Matthew lying in a pool of blood on the wooden floor. He wasn't moving. I dropped to my knees and searched for a pulse, and then lifted him up to find that the bullet had gone into his abdomen.

"Matthew, please no, god no"

I pulled at his shirt trying to ebb the flow of blood. It pulse through my hand as I held it firm.

"Jeanette, get help! Go get help!" I shouted as I pressed his shirt into the wound.

"They're already here," she replied

weakly as a team of Victorian police officers slammed open the door and rushed inside the clubs private room with their guns drawn.

"Don't shoot! Don't shoot!" Jeanette screamed as they aimed their guns at her.

"Please, he needs help, he's hurt." One of the policemen rushed to Eden, the other ran to Matthew.

"Please," I pleaded, hearing the desperation in my own voice. "Please, you need to help him." The officer spoke into his walkie talkie.

"We need a paramedics down here, immediately. White male with severe gunshot."

He looked at me. "Are you okay,

ma'am?"

"Please, he's dying. You have to help him, you need to do CPR or something on him, please, he needs help." The policeman looked at me, his eyes filled with sympathy.

"HELP HIM!" I screamed. Matthew wasn't moving.

The world started to spin as paramedics rushed into the room and began to work frantically on Matthew, pumping his chest.

"He's dead," I cried. "He's dead, isn't he?" But no one would answer me. The paramedics were working on Matthew, their hands moving in tandem as they tried to force life back into his body. I watched as one of them breathed into Matthew's mouth while the other one performed chest compressions, their movements perfectly choreographed.

"Ma'am, you need to come with me," the policeman who'd called for help said. "We need to get you out of here. You need medical attention." He had salt and pepper hair and a broad chest. His face was weathered, but his eyes were kind. The combination made me think he'd been around for a long time and seen a lot, that he'd been faced with the unthinkable.

"I can't leave him," I said. "I need to know if he's going to be okay." I was starting to get hysterical–I could hear it in my voice.

"You need to come with me so we can get you looked at," the officer said before he put his hand gently on my elbow and began leading me to the door.

I shook him off. "No,"

"No, I need to make sure he's okay."

"We have a pulse," one of the paramedics tending to Matthew said. I gasped in relief and began to cry, the sobs racking my body. But a second later, they brought in a stretcher and lifted Matthew onto it. His body was still lifeless, and the paramedic who'd announced Matthew's had a pulse jumped onto the stretcher and continued giving him chest compressions.

I felt like I could feel him slipping away. He'd been so pale, and there'd been so much blood.

If they'd found a pulse, why were they still doing CPR?

I started to follow the stretcher, but the policeman stepped in front of me. "Ma'am," he said. "Please, ma'am, you need to get checked out."

"I'm going with him." I pleaded.

"You can't go with him. There won't be any room in the ambulance."

A second set of paramedics loaded Eden onto a stretcher as Jeanette and I were taken down to the second ambulance. Meanwhile, the police secured the office and began their investigation.

A female paramedic stepped in front of me. "We're going to take you to the hospital to get checked out," the paramedic said.

She helped Jeanette and I up into the ambulance before closing the doors and taking off for the hospital. I held Jeanette's hand the whole ride to the hospital hoping that Matthew was still alive. Suddenly the fact that he'd lied and called me whore didn't matter. I love him and I can't bear to lose him.

Chapter 32

Jeanette

I knew she would think I was the victim, the stupid bitch. God, she even held my hand like I was some lost little girl. Yuck. I wasn't held captive; I was there to have things back the way they use to be. Me between Matthew and Eden. The way things should have been since they took my virginity. Me between the men I loved.

I had been a college freshman, when I met them. I'd been working at gala event as a waitress and tripped on the stairs with a tray full of glasses. If it hadn't of been for Matthew, I would have broken them all. He'd caught me and the tray sandwiching me between him and Eden. His words still fresh in my memory.

"Looks like we caught a one E, between us like all good girls should be." Remember drinking in his broad shoulders, dark hair and husky voice just like an aged whiskey. His warmth flushing through me. It was the man called "E" drew her a step back, until their bodies aligned, and I could feel his hard, thick, substantial erection pressing insistently against my bottom. I closed her eyes as a rush of moisture dampened my panties and my sex pulsed. I swallowed back a groan, struggling against the shameless urge to bend over, spread her legs, and beg him to fill her, take her.

"Are you okay there sweetheart, my big friend here, didn't scare you did he?" His voice full of laughter.

I wasn't scared no, it was a need of

desire that ran through me.

"Ha, no I'm more scared to lose this job then I am of you two." I forced myself to take the sarcastic tone like a shield to protect my true feelings.

"Did you hear that Matthew, not scared. That sounds like a challenge to me" E's breath hot against my ear.

I started to pull away and they let me go. "Um, thank you for saving me from falling. "

"It was our pleasure; I believe I will take that drink now though. How about you Eden?"

"I think I will, the gala may just be worth staying for after all."

That night was the first night

Matthew and Eden had shared me. It was the night I fell in love with two men. But that bitch came along and fucked everything up.

Eden had been the one to come up with the plan, he was the one to pay for the cosmetic surgery. I love my new look. New nose, chin and boobs sent guys wild. Matthew never seemed to notice though in the six months I had worked for him. I bit the inside of my lip just as I did anytime, I got upset. I will not give them the satisfaction of crying. No. I can't cry, it would mean I'm weak. I'm not going to let them get away with it. Matthew is mine and I'm going to take him back.

I still can't believe that they didn't notice it was me that put the abortion drugs into Sarah's coffee, just like Eden had planned. It was supposed to be the straw that broke the camel's back so to speak. It should have been the end of their marriage especially after we set up the scene at Highclere to make it sound like Eden had slept with Sarah. But no, the bitch still said she loved him. Well it's time to put an end to that. Let's see how much she loves him after I'm finished with him.

The End of Married Games

Want to see what happens to Sarah and Matthew and twisted games they are caught up in. Here's a sneak preview of Revenge Games.

Revenge Games

After finding out about her husband's past, Sarah realises that she knows nothing about the man she married. She is caught up in a game she didn't even know she was playing. The biggest question is, can she play for keeps?

Chapter 1

Matthew

"Oh shit," I groaned as I rose up through the layers of drug-induced sleep as pain flares through me.

"Fuck that hurts!"

"Shh, shh, lay still," the voice said moved around the room. I couldn't tell who it was because my eyes felt like they were glued shut and it took an enormous amount of effort to crack them open. When I did, everything was fuzzy, but I could feel a hand holding mine.

"What the hell happened?" I mumbled through cracked dry lips.

"You were shot," the voice said.

"How long have I been out?" I asked as I tried again to open my eyes and focus on my surroundings.

"Where am I?"

"You're in Monash Hospital in the ICU," the voice replied.

"You've been out for three days and we were beginning to really worry."

"Eh, I'm fine," I said as I struggled to try and move my arms. I wanted to sit up. I wanted to open my eyes and see what was going on around me. I wanted to know whose voice that was.

"No, no, no," the voice said gently holding my shoulder to the mattress. "You are not in any shape to be getting up, Mr. Davidson."

"Sarah, I need to find Sarah," I said suddenly remembering the events that had led to this point.

"Where is Sarah?"

"I'm right here, Matthew," Sarah whispered in my ear as she squeezed my hand. I opened my eyes and focused them on the face next to me. Her blue eyes were bright with tears as she gripped my hand more tightly and smiled.

"I'm right here. I'm not going anywhere."

"Oh, thank God, you're okay," I sighed as I felt the pain in my side begin to throb intensely. I groaned as Sarah tucked the button that released pain medication in my other hand and said, "Press it when you're in pain, it'll ease it."

I pressed the button and a few minutes later, I felt the pain begin to ease as I fell back into a groggy, half-wakeful state. I could feel Sarah's hand tucked in mine as I drifted back to sleep.

Chapter 2

Sarah

It had been two weeks since Matthew had been released from hospital. The police had been by and taken statements from Matthew, Jeanette and myself. I still couldn't believe that Eden had tried to kill us all. Most of all that it was all because he was in love with Matthew.

I had tried to be as attentive as I could. Making sure he rested and even disconnecting the home phone when his office continued to call over and over again. Jeanette his assistant had been amazing. She had managed his schedule and put off anything that wasn't urgent. Tomorrow though Matthew was supposed to return to work. Matthew didn't seem phased at all about it but something still felt off. I just couldn't put my finger on what it was. I was just glad that Jeanette would be there to take care of Matthew when I couldn't.

About J.F. Lowe

J. F. Lowe grew up in a country town in Central Queensland, Australia. With not much to do, it gave her plenty of time to create a fantasy world full of hot men and wild romances. Now living in Sydney, Australia when she's not writing, she can be found with a nice glass of wine and spends her time with her husband and holidaying with her three children.

J.F. Lowe loves romance and how it can be found in the strangest places. She truly believes in happily ever after.

J.F. Lowe also writes under her pen name of Nancy Drew - Author.

Connect with me online:

Website: www.jflowe.com

Facebook:

www.facebook.com/J.F.LoweAuthor

Instagram:

www.instagram.com/j.f.loweauthor

Twitter:

https://twitter.com/jflowe_author

BookBub:

https://www.bookbub.com/authors/j-f-

lowe

Keep in touch by engaging with me through one of the links above. Subscribe to my VIP Readers newsletter for exclusive excerpts.

http://www.jflowe.com/newsletter/

Series by J.F. Lowe

Married Games

Revenge Games (to be released June 11th, 2019)

Protecting Her Innocence (to be released July 2nd, 2019)

Series by Nancy Drew - Author

Masters of Highclere

A Sailors Daughter

Coxswains Cuffs

Returning to Highclere

Medical Ménage

Review

If you enjoyed this book, please review it or recommend it to others so they can find it, too.